I0524063

Mary Elizabeth Braddon

Taken at the Flood

A novel. Part 2

Mary Elizabeth Braddon

Taken at the Flood
A novel. Part 2

ISBN/EAN: 9783337050672

Printed in Europe, USA, Canada, Australia, Japan

Cover: Foto ©Andreas Hilbeck / pixelio.de

More available books at **www.hansebooks.com**

TAKEN AT THE FLOOD

A Novel

BY THE AUTHOR OF

'LADY AUDLEY'S SECRET'

ETC. ETC. ETC.

IN THREE VOLUMES

VOL. II.

LONDON

JOHN MAXWELL AND CO.

4 SHOE LANE, FLEET STREET

1874

LONDON:
PRINTED BY WOODFALL AND KINDER,
MILFORD LANE, STRAND, W.C.

CONTENTS TO VOL. II.

TAKEN AT THE FLOOD

CHAPTER I.

SIR AUBREY'S LAND STEWARD.

ONCE having taken the desperate leap which a few days ago he would have hardly believed it possible for him to take, Sir Aubrey was like a man caught in the web of some mystic enchantment. He was in feverish haste to make his bondage secure. The inward conviction that all the world—or all *his* world, which comes to the same thing—would secretly disapprove his new scheme of life, goaded him on to the completion of that act begun in a weak moment of bewilderment. Upon the path which he had taken delay seemed impossible.

'If I give these Hedingham and Monkhampton people time to talk about me, they will torment me to death,' he said to himself. ' The only plan is to be beforehand with them. My marriage cannot take place too soon.'

Sir Aubrey's world was a very small one, almost as small as Sylvia Carew's. Yet, there were some people in that small world about whose opinion he concerned himself not a little, notwithstanding that they were creatures of an inferior rank, whose approval or disapproval ought to have weighed lightly with him.

The two people of whom he thought most at this important crisis of his life were people whose very lives were, in a manner, dependent upon the light of his countenance. One was Shadrach Bain, his solicitor and land steward. The other was Jean Chapelain, his valet.

Half a century ago the family solicitors of the house of Perriam had been an old-established firm in Lincoln's-inn, men who ranked among the aristocracy of the legal profession, who did every thing in a grand, slow way, kept the title-deeds, wills, and marriage settlements of their clients in large iron safes that seemed inaccessible to man, so reluctantly were they opened, and who were altogether ponderous and respectable. Half a century ago, therefore, the lord of Perriam would have been outraged by the idea of employing a local solicitor. He had his land steward, or bailiff, a gentleman by birth and education, but not a lawyer; and all leases and contracts of whatever kind connected with the Perriam estate were drawn up and executed in their own tardy style by Messrs. Ferret and Tape of Lincoln's-inn. Sir Andrew Perriam, however, Sir Aubrey's father, had brought about a change in these things. He was a gentleman of close, and even miserly disposition, and soon after inheriting the property had discovered that the keenest pleasure he could derive from its possession would be found in its extension. He added a slip of woodland here, a field or two there, and, as the years crept by and his last map showed a widening boundary line to the lands of Perriam, felt that he had not lived in vain.

Sir Andrew speedily discovered that the gentleman land steward, who hunted three days a week in the season, and kept a pony carriage for his wife and daughters, was a mistake. He was not half sharp enough with the tenants, was much too ready to dip his hand into his employer's pocket for repairs and improvements, instead of squeezing everything out of the lessees; in fact, demoralized by his own easy life, he had become perniciously indulgent, and criminally indifferent to the interests of his employer. His salary was liberal, and he had thus an assured income, which underwent no diminution on account of a tenantless farm or a bankrupt tenant. This, Sir Andrew argued, was a radical error in the relations of master and steward. He had also a house rent free, and that the Perriam dower-house, a roomy old mansion of the Elizabethan order, which, with its ample gardens, orchards, and meadows, might have been let for two hundred a year. This, thought Sir Andrew, was a still greater mistake.

Having discovered this weakness in his business arrangements, Sir Andrew cast about him for a remedy, and was not slow to find one. The gentleman steward was dismissed with but a quarter's notice; the dower-house was let to a retired Monkhampton grocer; and Sir Andrew entrusted the collection of his rents, and the drawing up of leases and agreements, to Mr. Bain, an attorney at Monkhampton. This gentleman, shrewd, active, conciliating, and indefatigable, speedily contrived to establish a powerful influence over his employer. The Lincoln's-inn lawyers were ousted from their hold on the Perriam estate—the title-deeds, leases, and covenants wrested from their unwilling hands, and all the business that Sir Andrew had to give was given to Mr. Bain. When Sir Andrew made his will, it was Mr. Bain who drew up that document, Mr. Bain's clerks who witnessed its signature.

The uneventful years went by, and Sir Andrew slept the sleep of his forefathers, very well satisfied to his last hour with Mr. Bain's administration of the estate. Ten years after the death of his patron—the man who, in Monkhampton parlance, had made him—Mr. Bain was also gathered to his fathers, in their unpretending resting-place in the churchyard at Monkhampton. His son, a man of thirty, succeeded to the Perriam stewardship, and Sir Aubrey, who, with something of his father's love of money, had not inherited his father's business capacity, was glad to put his trust in an administrator whose management seemed always profitable to his employer. Shadrach Bain, the son, was, if anything, a better administrator than his father; for, from the time he left the Monkhampton Grammar School, at sixteen years of age, the Perriam estate had been the one all-absorbing thought of his mind. He knew it was the chief heritage to which he was to succeed. He knew that whatever his father might have saved out of his income had to be divided among a family of five,

two sons and three daughters, while the Perriam
stewardship was to descend, intact, to him the
eldest. There could be no division of that stewardship. Peter, the younger son, had been educated
at a local college for Baptist preachers, and
aspired to the honourable position of minister
in the little chapel in Water-lane, one of the
by-streets of Monkhampton. The Bains had been
Baptists almost from the establishment of that
sect.

Shadrach Bain knew every rood of ground within
the boundary of Sir Aubrey's land. From the
summit of a distant hill he could point with his
whip-handle to every bush, or knoll, or bank, or
poplar that indicated the dividing line between the
property of Sir Aubrey and his neighbouring land-
owners. 'My father negotiated the purchase of
yonder fallow,' he would say proudly; 'sixteen acres
two roods and three perches, and bought it uncommonly cheap. You see the three poplars at the
corner? That's our boundary. Nothing like
poplars to mark your line—grow quick and cast
very little shadow.'

He was a good farmer, Mr. Bain, though his
direct and personal experience of agriculture was
confined to the cultivation of a neat kitchen garden,

orchard, and meadow in the rear of his square, substantial dwelling-house in the High-street of Monkhampton. But he had read all the best books upon agriculture; before he was twenty he had made himself thoroughly acquainted with every improvement in agricultural implements; he had surveyed every farm within a day's journey of Monkhampton; had gone the round of the Perriam estate with his father as often as opportunity permitted; and, in keenness of vision, and clearness of comprehension and knowledge of the subject, was as good a farmer as he was a lawyer.

This man was now, for all practical purposes, master of the Perriam Manor.

Sir Aubrey knew about as much of farming or the capabilities of the estate, as he knew of the buried relics of Troja. So long as there was no fluctuation or falling off in his income, he was tolerably satisfied. His eye was pleased with the neat and picturesque appearance of the estate, as he rode his brown cob Splinter between the green banks of those sheltered lanes which intersected his domain. In one thing only did he and Mr. Bain differ. Sir Aubrey forbade the cutting down of a single tree, while Shadrach was, in his heart of hearts, for the stubbing-up system, and grumbled sorely at those fine old oaks and spreading beeches which made the beauty of the landscape, and soured the land beneath their dense leafage.

Things had gone well with Shadrach Bain. He had married young, and eminently to his own advantage ; though the Bain family affected to consider that Shadrach had condescended somewhat when he married Miss Dawker, eldest daughter of William Dawker, the Monkhampton grocer and provision dealer, who supplied all the surrounding unions and public institutions, and whose trade was altogether rather wholesale than retail.

Mr. Dawker had died shortly after his daughter's marriage, and Mrs. Bain inherited her portion of six thousand pounds sterling ; which, judiciously invested in cottage property, produced between four and five hundred a year. Shadrach was, therefore, in some measure, an independent man, and Monkhampton esteemed him accordingly. His house was one of the best in the town ; his garden a pattern of neatness ; his dog-cart fresh and bright as if newly come from the coach-builder's ; his horses—he never drove the same two days running—well groomed and cared for. His servants stayed with him year after year ; his children were well dressed, in a plain, substantial style, but with small regard to the mutations of fashion. His family pew in the Water-lane Chapel presented a picture of which Monk-hampton Baptists were proud.

Now, when Sir Aubrey Perriam thought of Sha-drach Bain, with his hard, commonplace method of coming at things, his rooted objection to the Orna-mental, his utter indifference to the Beautiful, and thought how such a man would receive the tidings of an intended marriage between a gentleman of fifty-seven years of age and a young lady of nine-teen, whose sole distinction, for vulgar minds, was her lovely face, his heart sank within him, and he felt that he would have a disagreeable business to go through when he announced to Mr. Bain the fact of his engagement with Sylvia Carew.

Yet, it would be necessary to acquaint his steward and solicitor with that fact before the marriage took place. Some kind of settlement there must be, though Sylvia was penniless. Mr. Bain was the person to draw up that settlement.

Jean Chapelain, the valet, was another individual who exercised a stronger influence over the mind of his master than Sir Aubrey would have cared to admit. An elderly bachelor, who keeps very little company, and passes some months of every year in the close quarters of a Parisian *entresol*, is apt to make his body-servant something of a companion. Chapelain's education was in advance of his position. He had read a good deal, in a desultory way, took a warm interest in European politics, and was, on the whole, a good deal better informed than his master. If Sir Aubrey wanted to talk, he could hardly talk to any one better worthy to be honoured with his conversation than the valet.

Thus, for the last twenty years, Jean Chapelain and his master had lived in close companionship. Into Jean's sympathetic ears Sir Aubrey had poured the elderly bachelor's philosophical reflections upon life and humanity. To Jean he had declared not once, but many times, that he valued the privileges of a single man far too well to barter them for the unknown joys of married life. Jean and he had laughed together at the folly of elderly Benedicts, the cynical laugh of men who had both drawn their views of life from that deep well of worldly wit and worldly wisdom, the writings of the most brilliant worldling the light ever shone upon, Voltaire.

To confess to Jean Chapelain that he had fallen in love and was going to marry the object of his affection, would be more humiliating even than to make the same confession to Shadrach Bain.

But happily, reflected Sir Aubrey, Chapelain need know nothing of the marriage till it was an accomplished fact. He could hardly grumble much then.

CHAPTER II.

MATTERS FINANCIAL.

Not a word did Sylvia say to her father all through that Sunday. He was at church almost all day with the school, so the two saw very little of each other in private. Indeed, under the pretext of a severe headache, Sylvia escaped her usual Sunday-school teaching, and afternoon and evening church, and contrived to spend the greater part of the day in the solitude of her own bedroom. There she could think in quiet; think, perhaps, very much as Judas may have thought before he went and hanged himself.

It is a kind of fate in some natures to betray. Falsehood is written in the stars that rule their destiny.

Sylvia thought of Mrs. Standen's indignation, and was angry with that lady for conduct which certainly appeared inconsistent.

' She ought to have thanked me for her son's release instead of turning upon me like that,' the girl said to herself, as she meditated upon that unpleasant scene with the lady who was to have been her mother-in-law.

After all, it was something to have got the interview over—to have cleared the ground for her new engagement. Who could tell how soon Hedingham might know of that wondrous change in her position? It would be her desire to keep the affair a secret as long as possible. But would Sir Aubrey or her father be likely to indulge this fancy of hers?

There remained the letter to be written to Edmund—the cruel, treacherous letter, in which, masking self-interest under an affectation of generosity, she was to give him up. His first letter to her had breathed only deepest trust and purest love. Her first letter to him would deal a death-blow to his dearest hopes.

Even though she was born to betray, it pained her to write that letter.

The composition was a work of art. It would have been difficult to read between the lines that told only of womanly forethought and self-abnegation, and to discover the mercenary spirit which prompted that renunciation. The letter seemed almost heroic. And here, truth assisted falsehood. The pangs with which Sylvia surrendered her lover were real enough. She did not forsake him without bitterest pain, harder to bear than the sorrow of an unselfish soul, which, out of pure magnanimity, foregoes its own joy.

The letter was written : and it was a relief to think that some time must elapse ere it could reach Edmund Standen's hands. The mail would only leave Southampton ten days hence. The passage of the letter to Demerara would take three weeks. There was breathing time therefore.

'Perhaps, being so entirely separated from me, and having leisure for reflection, he may have begun to regret his folly, and my letter may come to him almost as a relief,' thought Sylvia, self-excusingly.

On Monday evening the schoolmaster smoked his pipe in his favourite seat in the doorway—a narrow bench inside the latticed porch. The day had been rainy and the garden breathed the freshness and perfume that follow summer rain—sweet as incense rising from old Greek altars, when man knew no higher Giver of Good than Zeus or Demeter.

Sylvia had left her chair by the window, and had come, work in hand, to the doorway. She stood there, looking at her father curiously, as if doubtful whether to speak or be silent.

'Papa,' she said at last, 'you don't wish me to marry Mr. Standen?'

'Wish you to marry him!' exclaimed Mr. Carew, impatiently; 'why, you know that I have set my face against such a marriage, and that so far as a father can forbid anything, in these days of unfilial indifference to a father's wishes, I forbid you to marry Edmund Standen.'

'Even if Mrs. Standen were inclined to relent, papa, and to give a reluctant consent to the marriage, and leave Edmund half her fortune?'

'Is she inclined to do that?'

'Yes, papa. She called here yesterday, and told me so.'

Mr. Carew grew thoughtful.

'That might have altered the case considerably a week ago,' he said; 'but it only adds a perplexing element to the business now. I see a much more brilliant chance before you—if—if—the prospect is not delusive.'

'So do I, papa, looking at things from a worldly point of view.'

'From what other point of view need you look at things? We don't live in the stars!'

'Sir Aubrey Perriam has asked me to be his wife, papa.'

Mr. Carew started up from the little bench in the porch, and, for the first time within Sylvia's memory, dropped his pipe. It was a small meerschaum, coloured by himself, and he regarded it with an affection which he did not often bestow upon sentient things. He picked it up carefully, looked to see if he had chipped the bowl, and then stood staring at his daughter in silent amazement for some moments.

'Sir Aubrey asked you to marry him?' he said at last. 'In serious, sober earnest? It wasn't one of those senseless speeches which elderly gentlemen make to young ladies—mere old-fashioned gallantry —eh, Sylvia?'

'No, indeed, papa. I think Sir Aubrey was very much in earnest. His hand trembled a little when he took mine.'

'And you accepted him?' said the father sharply.

He was prepared for any folly from a girl of nine-teen. It is in the nature of youth to be sentimental; and he supposed that his daughter must have the ordinary share of sentimentality.

'Yes, papa. I was engaged to Edmund Standen, but everything seemed to be against our marriage, so I thought——'

'You were wise, for once in your life,' cried Mr. Carew. 'Why, you will be a queen, child. And I —well, I suppose I shall not be compelled to end my days as a parish schoolmaster. Why didn't you tell me this before? Has my life been such a bright one that you need keep the sunshine of prosperity from me?'

'I—I—hardly knew how to tell you, papa. Poor Edmund. It seems so hard to give up every thought of him.'

'Well, it's rather a sudden renunciation, certainly. However, no girl in her senses would act otherwise than you have done. Rather lucky that your sweetheart was off to Demerara.'

'Yes, papa. I don't think I could have accepted Sir Aubrey if Edmund had not been away.'

'I suppose Sir Aubrey means to explain himself to me to-morrow.'

'I think he is coming here to-night, papa.'

'Then you had better clear out of the way. We must have our talk alone.'

'Very well, papa. I'll go to Mary Peter's. I want to see the dress she's making for Miss Jane Toynbee. Oh, how nice it will be when I have new dresses of my own! Oh, by-the-bye, papa, if Sir Aubrey should want to fix the date of our marriage—

he would hardly wish to do that yet awhile, but if he should—make it as far off as you can. I don't want the Standens quite to despise me, as they would if they knew that I had jilted Edmund in order to marry Sir Aubrey.'

'Defer the marriage! Yes, and give Sir Aubrey time to alter his mind, or to die in the interval; and then you would realize the old adage of "between two stools." No, Sylvia; if Sir Aubrey wishes for a short engagement I shall not be insane enough to propose delay.'

Sylvia sighed, thought of all the joys that must attend the translation from poverty to wealth, and submitted. She put on her hat, and ran off to spend half an hour among the cuttings of silk and lining and open papers of pins which bestrewed Mary Peter's humble apartment on a busy evening. What would poor Mary Peter say if she heard of this new engagement? There had been talk enough and astonishment enough about Edmund Standen's subjugation. But this latter conquest was as far above the first as yonder evening star, shining softly above the cypress, surpasses the feeble lustre of village lamps. Sylvia did not mean to tell her humble confidante about the change in her circumstances yet awhile.

Mr. Carew had not been alone ten minutes before

he heard the click of the latch, and the garden gate opened to admit Sir Aubrey Perriam. The schoolmaster had been wondering, with sore perplexity, whether that proposal, whereof Sylvia had just informed him, had been really a serious offer, or only one of those florid meaningless compliments which gentlemen of the old school are apt to indulge in.

The sight of that gray-haired figure in the summer dusk set his heart beating at a gallop. The whole thing had seemed too good to be true. But this appearance of the baronet seemed to confirm Sylvia's statement.

James Carew emptied the ashes out of his pipe, and dropped that treasure into the pocket of his well-worn velveteen shooting jacket as Sir Aubrey came up the garden path.

' Good evening, Mr. Carew,' said the visitor, in his low bland tones. ' All alone ? Miss Carew is out, I suppose,' he added, looking into the parlour through the wide open casement.

' Yes, Sylvia has gone to see one of her friends in the village. She has very few friends, poor child ; and the one or two she does associate with are hardly congenial spirits. But my poor girl has a soft, clinging nature, and must have something to love.'

' I regret to lose the pleasure of seeing her,' said

Sir Aubrey, ' yet I am not sorry she is absent. I wish to have a little serious talk with you, Mr. Carew. Your daughter has told you the motive of this visit, perhaps ? '

' She hinted at something, which I could hardly believe possible. I thought my poor child, in utter ignorance of the world, might naturally mistake gallantry for—for——'

' For affection,' said Sir Aubrey. ' I am not skilled in the art of gallantry, Mr. Carew, and when I spoke to your daughter the other night—too hastily, perhaps—I spoke straight from my heart.'

' And your words went straight to hers, Sir Aubrey,' answered the schoolmaster with feeling. ' Need I say how deeply I feel the honour you have conferred upon my daughter. Yet when I reflect upon the disparity——'

' In our ages ? ' said Sir Aubrey quickly.

' No, Sir Aubrey, in your social position. If I objected to my daughter's union with a banker's son, whose family opposed the marriage—have I not still stronger reason to object to a marriage which all the county will condemn ? '

' Do you imagine, sir, that I exist only to please my neighbours ? ' cried Sir Aubrey haughtily. ' The lady I choose for my wife, sir, ascends at once to my own level, and let me see any gentleman or lady in this county who will presume to disparage her. Come, Mr. Carew, let us discuss this subject from a business point of view. I have proposed for your daughter's hand, and she has done me the honour to accept me without reserve. The preliminaries of the marriage are all that you and I have to settle.'

' Will you take a seat, Sir Aubrey, and allow me to light the candles?' said Mr. Carew, leading the way into the dusky parlour.

' You needn't light candles. We can talk just as well in the twilight,' said the visitor, seating himself just within the doorway.

Mr. Carew was not sorry to remain in that friendly half-light. Who could tell what questions the baronet might intend to ask him—questions upon which his daughter's future fortunes might depend—questions which might tax his ingenuity to the uttermost to answer satisfactorily? It was some advantage to keep his face in the shadow.

' When a man of my age makes such a proposal as I have made to your daughter,' began Sir Aubrey, ' it is only natural to suppose that he is moved by a deep and powerful feeling. I have heard of love as swift and sudden as this love of mine, and ridiculed it, many a time before to-day. I now confess, in all

humility, that I underrated the power of the god.
He has avenged himself upon my infidelity, and has
transformed the unbeliever into a fanatic.'

He paused, sighed gently, as if regretting his own
abasement, and then went on in the same half-medi-
tative tone.

'You say the county, which has its own standard
of right, will take objection to my marriage with
your daughter. I am prepared for that. I will go
further and say I know that they will ridicule my
infatuation—set me down as a dotard, at fifty-seven
years of age—laugh at the old man and his fair
young wife. In answer to all this I can only say
that I know my own heart, and that it is not mere
admiration for your daughter's beauty which has
influenced my conduct. I should despise myself
could I think that I had been caught by a pretty
face; like the brainless moth which seeks its de-
struction in the flame that dazzles and allures it.
No, Mr. Carew, I love your daughter honestly, and
sincerely, in all purity and truth; and I am willing
to trust the remnant of my days to her keeping.'

'Nay, Sir Aubrey, at fifty-seven a man has hardly
passed the prime of life.'

'Have you any objection to offer to this marriage,
sir?' asked Sir Aubrey, with a stately condescen-

sion; as if fully aware that the question was an empty courtesy.

'Objection! I **am** deeply honoured by your choice. I feel more pride than I can venture to express, lest I should appear servile.'

'**Not another word, Mr. Carew.** I feel that, however humble your present position may be, you were born to occupy a better one.'

'**I was, Sir Aubrey.** My father was a merchant of some standing, who sent me to Eton and Oxford, and suffered me to marry and begin life with the idea that I was a man of independent means. His failure and death within **three years of my** poor Sylvia's birth left me a pauper. This employment, humble though it is, was the best that offered itself to the ruined Oxonian, who had neither trade nor profession. You may say, perhaps, that I might in all these years have endeavoured to improve my condition. I can only answer that whatever energies I ever had were deadened by the blow which reduced **me from** delusive affluence to actual poverty. The **little I can earn** here has sufficed to maintain **my** child and **myself.** The retired life has suited my habits and inclinations; and thus I have never taken arms against **a sea of** troubles, but have rather preferred the obscurity of this peaceful haven.'

'I understand,' said Sir Aubrey. 'And you had no wife to share or lighten your struggles. She died before your misfortunes?'

'Yes, my wife was dead.'

'I inferred as much.'

There was a pause. Sir Aubrey had something more to say, but hardly knew how to say it. He was a rich man, and he had told himself that this Mr. Carew might entertain an exaggerated notion of a wealthy bridegroom's liberality. He might count upon profiting to some large extent by his daughter's union with the lord of the manor. It was for Sir Aubrey to undeceive him at once upon this point.

'Your daughter having done me the honour to accept me, and there being no impediment to our marriage, it appears to me, Mr. Carew, that the event cannot take place too soon: unless, indeed, Sylvia should desire delay; a wish which I should infinitely regret, for where there is so great a disparity of years that wish might indicate uncertainty of purpose.'

'My daughter has no such wish, Sir Aubrey,' replied Mr. Carew promptly: 'but a woman can hardly pass from the position of my daughter to that of your wife without some trifling preparations in the way of *trousseau*.'

'Of course. But in all her arrangements I hope Miss Carew will remember that I am a man of the simplest habits; that I see hardly any society, and that I utterly abhor the frivolities of fashion.'

'I have no doubt that she will be proud to be ruled by your superior judgment in all things,' replied the schoolmaster, who was beginning to feel a shade of anxiety. There had been, so far, not a syllable that hinted at any improvement in his own circumstances. Sir Aubrey had not uttered the important word settlement. And it was a word which Mr. Carew felt could hardly issue from his lips. To betray his expectation of profit from the marriage would seem like bargaining for the price of his daughter.

While he was meditating this, somewhat uncomfortably, Sir Aubrey relieved his doubts by becoming business-like.

'With regard to settlements,' he said, 'I conclude that as you can give nothing to your daughter, you will not entertain any exaggerated expectations upon that point. I will freely own to you that I do not understand or approve the modern system of making a wife independent of her husband. Dependence is one of woman's sweetest attributes— her most winning charm. I should not like my wife—were she a nobleman's daughter—to possess an independent income during my lifetime. I shall, therefore, settle nothing upon Sylvia.'

Mr. Carew's heart grew heavy. Why, at this rate Edmund Standen might have been a better match than Sir Aubrey.

' But I shall settle two or three thousand a year upon my widow. When I die Sylvia shall have that income, and the dower-house—now let off, and worth two hundred a year.'

' Sir Aubrey,' said the schoolmaster with a dignified air, ' far be it from me to dispute the justice or the generosity of any decision you may arrive at. I am certainly inclined to think that for my daughter's future comfort, and your exemption from small worries, it might have been wise for you to settle upon her some moderate allowance in the way of pin-money, were it only three or four hundred a year, which would have made her independent, so far as concerns a woman's trifling requirements.'

' A woman's trifling requirements,' echoed Sir Aubrey; ' you don't mean to tell me that your daughter, brought up in this cottage, would require three or four hundred a year to buy gowns and bonnets ? '

' Certainly not, Sir Aubrey. But charity makes a

large item in a lady's expenditure, and Sylvia, as the mistress of Perriam, could hardly come to you for every half-crown she wanted to give to a sick cottager.'

'Good heavens, sir,' cried the baronet, 'do you suppose that I cannot make my wife an allowance for pocket-money, when she is my wife, without binding myself to pay her so many hundreds a year upon a piece of stamped parchment before I marry her? I will amply provide for your daughter in the event of my death; but I will never consent to render her independent of my bounty during my lifetime.'

The schoolmaster murmured a vague assent; but felt more and more uncomfortable. 'How am I to profit by such a marriage?' he wondered. 'Am I to sit in the gate like Mordecai, and to be not a jot better off for my daughter's advancement?'

Again Sir Aubrey came to his relief.

'As regards yourself, Mr. Carew,' he began, graciously, 'I have reflected that it could hardly be satisfactory to you to occupy your present position—honourable as that position is—when your daughter is Lady Perriam. I shall therefore request you to accept a hundred a year, which I shall be very happy to remit to you by quarterly payments, in lieu of your present stipend, and which will enable you to live in quiet independence——' the baronet was about to say 'elsewhere,' but checked himself lest the phrase should sound like a sentence of banishment, —' in any locality most agreeable to yourself.'

' You are very good, Sir Aubrey. I place my future entirely at your disposal,' answered the schoolmaster.

' A hundred a year! A poor pittance, although twice as good as my present income,' he thought, deeply disappointed by the baronet's narrow views on the subject of settlements. He had fancied that an elderly lover would be lavish—ready to empty his coffers at the feet of his idol. And here was Sir Aubrey, driving as hard a bargain as if he had been Shadrach Bain cheapening a herd of store oxen at Monkhampton cattle fair.

A hundred a year! It seemed a pitiful result of such a wondrous event as the baronet's subjugation. Mr. Carew could only comfort himself with the idea that Sylvia, once married, must assuredly acquire some power over her husband's purse, and that it would be hard if her father were not something the better for her altered fortunes.

' You spoke just now of Sylvia's *trousseau*,' said Sir Aubrey, who felt more at his ease now that he had expounded his views. 'I have **not** forgotten that necessity. Perhaps you will contrive **to give** your daughter this little packet without offending her **delicacy.** **It contains a** hundred pounds in bank-**notes.'**

James Carew took the small parcel, and his faded face flushed faintly at the mere thought of its con-**tents.** How long **it was** since he **had** held as much money in his hand! **The day had been when a** hundred pounds would **have** made an insignificant **item in** the vast sum of his needs; but of late years sovereigns had been as drops of his heart's blood, so dear had it cost him to part with them.

'I shall be obliged **if you bear in mind what I** said just **now about** simplicity of **attire,'** said Sir Aubrey, when Mr. **Carew** had murmured his ac-knowledgment of the **lover's** first gift. '**A** woman **cannot** be too plainly dressed **for** my taste; **nor** does Sylvia's beauty need adornment.'

Sylvia opened the gate while her elderly **lover was** speaking, and came across the dusky garden. Sir Aubrey went out **to meet** her, almost as eager as **if he had been** twenty-five instead of fifty-seven. Business-like and deliberate as he had been in the adjustment of monetary questions, **he became en-**thusiastic at sight of Sylvia.

'My sweet one,' he said, detaining her in the garden, ' I have seen your father, and settled everything. And now I want you to name the happy day that is to make us one.'

That sudden appeal made Sylvia tremble. What, was her doom so near? She had thought it a grand thing to be Lady Perriam while that change of fortune appeared still distant. She had forsworn herself—renounced her lover—become a renegade. Yet at the near approach of that brilliant fortune for which she had sacrificed all lesser things, there came a revulsion of feeling. If she could by any possibility have drawn back at this last moment she would have done it, recalled her renunciation of Edmund, become once more the happy girl who had pillowed her head upon her lover's breast and felt herself brave enough to face even poverty for his sake.

But it was all too late for turning back. Sir Aubrey's patrician hand had drawn hers gently through his arm with an air of proprietorship.

' Let it be as soon as possible, my dear,' he said, in a tone that was half lover-like, half fatherly; ' the autumn will soon be upon us, and I should like to spend September in Paris. I am always glad to get away from the falling leaves.'

Paris seemed a name of enchantment to this un-travelled girl. Not Damascus, Bassora, or Bagdad —no city she had ever read of in the Arabian Nights —could have more the sound of a fairy tale.

'I should like to see Paris,' she said, forgetting her tardy remorse.

'We will spend our honeymoon there, love!' replied the baronet, who had made up his mind about it before he came to woo. It would be an inexpensive honeymoon. Lodgment in his *entresol* would cost him nothing. There would only be some slight difference in the terms of his contract with the *traiteur* who supplied his table.

'Your father agrees with me that there is no motive for delay, except for the brief time you may require to have two or three dresses made,' said Sir Aubrey. 'We will be married very quietly in yonder church some morning, before any of the village gossips have had time to discover our inten-tion.'

'That will be nice,' said Sylvia, somewhat list-lessly, 'but I should have liked a few months' delay.'

'A few months! What for?'

The question was embarrassing.

'How can you be sure that you really care for me

—that your regard for me is anything more than a passing fancy ?' she faltered after a pause.

'I have no doubt as to *my* feelings,' replied Sir Aubrey, with offended dignity ; 'perhaps it is you who are doubtful about yours.'

'No, indeed!' cried Sylvia quickly. Not for worlds must she offend him. Was not the die cast? She might keep back her letter to Edmund, which was not yet posted, but she could not undo her interview with Mrs. Standen. The next mail would doubtless carry a full account of that interview to her lover. And was it likely he would forgive her for having rejected his mother's offered friendship— for having renounced him deliberately in the very hour of his mother's relenting? Sylvia felt that Edmund was lost to her, and that there was nothing for her between marriage with Sir Aubrey and igno- minious downfall.

Reflection showed her that her own interest de- manded a speedy marriage. What would be her position if Edmund came back and denounced her ? He might be cruel enough to tell Sir Aubrey how fondly she had loved him ; with what oft-repeated vows she had sworn to be true. What might not a betrayed lover do to proclaim her baseness ? The best possible shelter would be Sir Aubrey's name.

No one would dare to **assail or to insult Sir Aubrey** Perriam's wife.

' Come, Sylvia,' said the baronet tenderly, ' if you love me ever so little you will not ask for delay. It is in your power to make my life very happy. Why should not my happiness begin as soon as it can ? Remember, my sweet one, when you accepted my offer the other night you linked your life with mine. You can hardly unlink it again, unless you really repent your promise.'

'No, no. I do not repent. I am honoured, proud, happy, in the knowledge of your love.'

' Then we will be married **this day month,**' said Sir Aubrey, sealing the bond with a courteous kiss.

Sylvia made no objection. It is not for the beggar girl to dictate to King Cophetua.

CHAPTER III.

SIR AUBREY, always an early riser, breakfasted a little earlier than usual on the morning after his interview with Sylvia, and mounted his favourite Splinter directly after breakfast, to ride into Monkhampton. The day was dull and cloudy, and the landscape had not its usual smile as he walked his horse along the hilly road between Perriam and the market town.

Rather a quiet place, Monkhampton, at this hour of the morning. There were two or three sleek vestrymen lounging near the door of that uninviting building the Vestry Hall, disputing about sewer rates, and the advisability or non-advisability of an additional twopence in the pound, lately a point in discussion. The bells were ringing for a week-day service, and a few respectable matrons and a sprinkling of young ladies might be seen wending

their way to the parish church; but commerce
seemed to be hardly awake in Monkhampton at a
quarter-past ten in the morning.

Sir Aubrey drew rein at a house near the beginning
of the High-street, in a neighbourhood where the
town touched the border of the country, and where
the houses boasted larger gardens than in the heart
of Monkhampton. The house before which the
baronet stopped was strong, and solid, and square,
and respectable—a house which insolvency could
never have inhabited, one might fancy, so boldly did
it stare the world in the face—so aggressive was the
look of its tall iron railings. It was built of dull,
yellow bricks, picked out with red, and had three
rows of windows, five in a row on the two upper
floors, two on each side of the hall door. The steps
were as white as hearthstone could make them; the
windows as bright as if they had been cleaned that
morning, but no flower-pot, no birdcage, no frivolity
of any kind decorated those windows. The two on
the left of the door were draped with crimson curtains of a substantial moreen, that assumed the
stiffest, straightest folds possible to a textile fabric;
the windows on the right were screened as to the
lower panes by wire blinds, stern barriers against
the prying gaze of passers-by, blinds which said as

plain as words could speak, 'We guard the sanctity of a lawyer's office.'

On the large brass plate, which gave additional dignity to the stout oak street door, appeared the following inscription :—

Mr. Shadrach Bain,
Solicitor and Land Agent.

Sir Aubrey gave Splinter to his groom, turned the brazen handle of Mr. Bain's door, and went in without further ceremony.

The houses in Monkhampton were, as a rule, thus accessible to the public, and Sir Aubrey was familiar with the habits of his agent. The door on the right of the entrance had the word 'Office' painted on its panels, in severe-looking black letters. This door Sir Aubrey opened, and confronted his land steward, who was seated at a desk opposite the door, plodding through a lease with a pencil in his mouth, ready to take note of any flaw in the agreement.

Shadrach Bain was a man of that doubtful and indefinite age which is sometimes called the prime of life. Time had as yet traced no wrinkle on the land steward's brow, amply provided with those organs of calculation and perception which assist the pursuit of gain. His hard gray eyes had the clear brightness of perfect health ; his dark brown hair still thickly thatched his head; his complexion had a ruddy brownness, not unpleasant to the eye— a hue that told of long rides in the fresh morning air rather than of the midnight lamp. He was tall, broad-shouldered, well built, and, like the Miltonian Satan, stood like a tower among his fellow men. He dressed well, but cultivated rather the outward aspect of a small squire than the sombre attire of the learned professions. He liked, when he went a little beyond his own beat, to be hailed as 'Squire' by railway porters and the commonalty. He had bushy brown whiskers, a close-shaved lip and chin, wore a suit of heather tweed, a blue cravat, and a plaited leather watch-chain.

He rose briskly at sight of his patron, wheeled forward the one comfortable chair of the office, and shut a door which communicated with an inner room, whence the scratching of the clerks' pens had been audible as the baronet entered.

'This is an unexpected honour, Sir Aubrey,' he said in a cheery tone, as the baronet shook hands with him. Sir Aubrey did not always greet his agent so warmly—there were times when he appeared to consider a friendly nod sufficient, and Mr. Bain never invited more familiarity than his patron offered. He took condescensions from Sir

Aubrey as wise heathens took the gifts of the gods.
But to-day his employer was more than commonly
cordial, and Mr. Bain augured that there was something in the wind. '*I* breakfast at seven all the
year round,' said Mr. Bain, as his visitor settled
himself in the arm-chair; 'but one doesn't expect
to see you in Monkhampton before noon.'

'I came early because I've something rather
particular to say to you, Bain,' answered the baronet,
playing with the tassel of his riding whip. 'I don't
suppose it'll surprise you, for it was a thing to
be anticipated sooner or later. For although a
man has come to—ahem—between fifty and sixty—
there's no necessity for him to spend all his days in
solitude.'

Shadrach Bain dropped his pencil, and looked at
his employer steadily with those penetrating eyes of
his—those gray orbs which, with little expression
except keenness, seem to have more seeing power
than any other eyes. Mr. Bain began to wonder if
the baronet might not be just a little weak in his
head, like Mordred, who was popularly supposed to
be not quite rational. His mind was beginning to
fail, perhaps, poor old gentleman, and he was thinking of going into a monastery, or turning Plymouth
Brother.

' There needn't be much solitude at Perriam, Sir Aubrey,' said Mr. Bain. 'People would be glad enough to come and see you if you asked them. Though I don't say but what hospitality, or keeping open house, as people call it, would make away with no end of money; money which would be better employed in enlarging the estate, as Sir Andrew did before you. There's the Combe farm must come into the market when old Parker dies—it joins our land at Wapshot, you know, Sir Aubrey—and would be a very nice addition to your property.'

'We'll talk about Combe when it is in the market,' replied Sir Aubrey, with a touch of offended dignity. He thought his steward ought to have been quicker to understand him. 'I am not talking of county society. Of course I could fill my house with people if I chose, and, as you say, squander a great deal of money upon visitors who would hardly thank me for my hospitality. But I don't at all desire society of that kind. When I spoke just now of solitude, I meant the solitude of a bachelor. The only companionship I wish for is that of a wife I could love.'

The baronet pronounced the last word reluctantly. No girl of seventeen could have uttered the portentous syllable more coyly.

Mr. Bain's countenance changed not at this announcement. Very early in life had Mr. Bain brought his facial muscles into complete subjection. They were too well trained to betray him. But his broad, strong hand gripped the rail of his chair with a somewhat savage grasp. The hand was behind his back, and Sir Aubrey could not see the action.

'You have some idea of marrying?' said Mr. Bain, with a smile, that cold smile which comes and goes at the bidding of the smiler, chill as wintry sunlight.

'I have more than an idea, Shadrach. I am going to be married on the twentieth of August.'

'Next August?'

'Of course. Do you suppose I'm going to put my wedding off for a year. What need I wait for?'

'Nothing, certainly—as regards pecuniary arrangements. But this seems uncommonly sudden. You have known the lady a long time no doubt.'

'I have known her long enough to love her.'

'Should I be impertinent if I asked who she is?'

'Not at all. I came this morning to arrange the question of a settlement. But you understand, Bain, that what a man tells his solicitor is sacred.'

'Of course.'

'The fact is I don't want any one in Monkhampton

to know that I'm going to be married. I don't want the affair to be so much as suspected till it's all over. I hate talk and fuss, and to be stared at or whispered about. No doubt people will be surprised at my marriage; but they can have their fill of surprise while I **am away for my honeymoon, and** get accustomed to the fact before I **come back.'**

'There **is hardly any** occasion **for** surprise, Sir Aubrey, except at the suddenness of the business,' said Mr. Bain, with his most deferential air. 'The match is a suitable one, no doubt.'

'I'll trouble you to reserve **your doubts** and your speculations till you know all about it,' resumed the baronet testily. '**The** match is **not** what society may **call suitable.** The match is what the world generally **ridicules in** young or old—a love match. The young lady—a lady in everything **except posi-**tion—is beneath me in station.'

'Old idiot! He has fallen in love with some pretty housemaid, or a circus rider, or a French actress,' thought Mr. Bain, not yet relaxing his **grasp of the chair rail.**

'The young lady is the only daughter of Mr. Carew, the parish schoolmaster at Hedingham,' said Sir Aubrey.

' The parish schoolmaster's daughter ! Why, that's the young lady whom young Standen was sweet upon. My daughter Matilda Jane heard something about it at the Hedingham Fancy Fair.'

' I beg leave to suggest that " sweet upon" is not a phrase I care to hear in relation to my future wife,' remonstrated the baronet stiffly. ' I am fully aware that Mr. Standen wished to marry Miss Carew, and was rejected by her father.'

' He rejected Edmund Standen, of Dean House ! That's curious. However, if the young lady was engaged to you, Sir Aubrey, that explains matters.'

' She was not engaged to me at the time of Mr. Standen's proposal. That young man's offer was rejected on its own merits.'

' Indeed. Well, I hope my daughters may be as lucky when their time comes.'

' You are perhaps not aware that Miss Carew is a young lady of exceptional beauty,' said Sir Aubrey with ever-increasing stiffness ; ' a lady who might have won the affections of a gentleman of even more exalted position than my own.'

' She is very young, I suppose ?'

' Between nineteen and twenty.'

' I should have thought, whatever the merits of

the lady, a somewhat longer engagement would have been advisable. Of course, I don't presume to offer my advice, Sir Aubrey.'

'Sir,' returned the baronet, with a freezing look, 'this is a matter in which I ask advice from no man.'

Mr. Bain murmured an apology. Sir Aubrey recovered his temper. He felt elated even, for he felt that he had put down Mr. Bain. He had come to that office not without trepidation, had felt himself blushing as he rode along the empty lanes, and he was glad to think that he had been able to assert himself thus boldly.

'Now, with regard to the settlement,' he said, with his usual friendliness of manner. 'I have come to the determination to settle nothing upon my wife during my lifetime. If her affection for me be as sincere as I venture to consider it, she will be content to owe all to my bounty. She will not want to squander my money. To settle an income upon her for her own separate use would be in a manner to instil extravagance.'

'True, Sir Aubrey,' said Mr. Bain with approval, 'but in that case I don't see that you want a settlement at all.'

'You forget the disparity of years between Miss

Carew and myself. I am bound to provide for her after my death.'

'You could do that by will.'

'Certainly. But I prefer to make her future secure by an immediate settlement. I gratify myself by leaving her dependent upon my liberality so long as I live, but I wish to show myself capable of generosity——'

'After death,' said Mr. Bain, finishing the sentence.

'My wife will look to me for all she needs, but I shall amply provide for the independence of my widow,' returned the baronet.

'I understand. Then we have only to settle what portion of your estate you will charge with this provision. You would be able to leave Lady Perriam —how much?'

'I have been thinking that two thousand a year——' said Sir Aubrey meditatively.

'A poor provision for a lady accustomed to the occupation of Perriam.'

'I do not spend more than four thousand at Perriam.'

'Perhaps not—but after your marriage things will be different. Where you now spend four thousand, I daresay you'll spend ten.'

Sir Aubrey shook his head.

' I beg your pardon,' he said. ' There will be no difference. A man doesn't change his habits after fifty. Were I to marry a fashionable young woman —accustomed to the dissipations of the London season—I might be expected to alter my mode of living—to launch out in some absurd manner—re-furnish Perriam with your tawdry modern rubbish— set up a house in town—and so on. But I marry a young lady who has no pretensions—who is simply the loveliest girl I ever saw—a violet which hides itself in the shelter of its leaves—as somebody once remarked of some one else. What Perriam has been in the past, Perriam will continue to be in the future —until it passes to its next possessor.'

' Your son, perhaps,' suggested Mr. Bain, who had been thinking profoundly while Sir Aubrey ex-pounded his views. That strong Saxon face looked almost handsome when the man thought. There was such strength of purpose in it. The clear, gray eyes clouded, as the man's gaze—no longer pene-trating the surface of actual things—surveyed those impalpable shadows which make the vision of things to be.

' My son. If God blesses me with children,' replied Sir Aubrey reverently.

'I don't think two thousand is enough for a man in your position to leave his widow,' said Mr. Bain presently

He was to some extent a privileged person, and could speak as plainly as he chose to Sir Aubrey. He had frequent occasion to demonstrate that he knew the baronet's interests a great deal better than the baronet himself understood them, and had thus acquired a certain empire over the weaker brain of his employer.

'Two thousand a year is a large income for Mr. Carew's daughter,' said Sir Aubrey thoughtfully.

'But a paltry pittance for Sir Aubrey Perriam's widow,' returned the other. 'Why should you stint this lady? You love her; and if she brings you no children, all you do not leave to her will go to your distant relative—a man for whom you don't care two straws.'

'Not one,' said Sir Aubrey.

'The bulk of the estate is entailed, and must go to Mr. Horace Perriam—after your brother's death that is to say—and his life is not so good as your own. But there's a large remainder that is not in the entail—all the land bought by Sir Andrew, and the Warren estate, which you inherited from your mother. Why not act handsomely towards this lady in the matter of a future provision? Why not leave her five thousand a year, chargeable on the Warren estate and on the Felldrake and the Coppice farms?'

Sir Aubrey opened his eyes in a blank stare. He had expected all kinds of opposition from Shadrach Bain, and most of all had he expected to be opposed in the matter of the settlement, and here was Shadrach Bain pleading the cause of the future Lady Perriam, a person he had never seen, if his own statement were to be trusted.

'Five thousand a year for a schoolmaster's daughter,' said the baronet feebly.

'Five thousand a year for Lady Perriam,' replied the steward. 'If she is worthy of your confidence and your affection, she is worthy of your liberality. Most men in my position would look at this question from the solicitor's point of view, and counsel meanness. I recommend liberality. If you have no children, strangers—or those who are no nearer to you than strangers—will come after you. Why should you pinch the wife of your choice to fatten strangers? You cannot be too generous to Lady Perriam—after your death.'

'True,' murmured Sir Aubrey, impressed by this mode of argument, 'I shall be none the poorer. It will make no difference to me in my grave whether she has two thousand or five thousand. But, if the dead are capable of thinking about the world they leave behind them, it *would* vex me to think that Horace Perriam had everything.'

'Of course it would. Shall I draw up a draft of the deed of settlement, and bring it to Perriam Place this evening?'

'Yes, bring it this evening. Mr. Carew and his daughter are to dine with me, by the way. Don't say anything about it before them. I might change my mind as to the amount. After all, it would be always in my power to provide for my widow by will. The settlement is only a matter of form, to satisfy the father, who no doubt wants to see his daughter's future secured.'

'If you doubt the lady, make no settlement,' said Mr. Bain decisively. 'If you believe in her, make her a handsome one.'

'Believe in her!' cried the baronet, flashing out indignantly; 'do you suppose I should marry her if I did not believe her to be all that is good and pure and high-minded?'

'You have known her so short a time!'

'Sir, there are intuitions,' exclaimed Sir Aubrey solemnly.

'Then settle the five thousand, and back your opinion, as the racing men say.'

'So be it—draw up the draft, and let me have it for consideration. There will be plenty of time for execution between this and the marriage. Oh, by the bye, there's one document you can make as plain and brief as you please—an agreement promising to pay Mr. James Carew a hundred a year, in quarterly instalments, during the remainder of his life. I can't have my father-in-law a parish schoolmaster. I give him a maintenance which will support him in comfort and decency for the rest of his days. Perhaps you'll ask me to make it five hundred,' added the baronet, with some asperity.

'No, Sir Aubrey. A hundred a year for the father I consider ample. I hope I have not offended by my regard for the interests of the future Lady Perriam.'

'No, Bain. You're a good fellow, I know, and devoted to your employer, as your father was before you. I like you for taking Miss Carew's part. I'm obliged to you. I thought you would have echoed that parrot-cry about disparity of years, unsuitability of tempers, and so on. I like you for taking my future wife's part against me. Why should the heir-at-law get more than he is strictly entitled to ?

He'll get the benefit of all my father's improvements on the estate proper—Gad—he shall have not an acre of the land we've added. I'll settle five thousand on Sylvia, and I daresay I shall leave her a good deal more if she makes me as good a wife as I believe she will. Good-day, Bain, you may as well come to dinner, by the way—come at six, and we shall have an hour for going through the settlement before the Carews arrive.'

Mr. Bain professed himself happy to obey any commands of Sir Aubrey. He generally dined at Perriam once or twice a year, when there was some odd bit of land in the market, or some important lease to be renewed. The invitation was understood to be a condescension on Sir Aubrey's part, despite Mr. Bain's professional status and legal right to the title of gentleman. Mrs. Bain had never been invited with her husband, and in Mrs. Bain's particular circle the baronet was set down as a proud man.

' He wouldn't have the income he has if it wasn't for Bain,' the lady would observe to her gossips, ' but he hasn't a spark of gratitude in his nature. He'll take off his hat to me in my own hall as politely as a Sir Chesterfield Walpole, but never so much as open his lips to wish me good morning.'

Mr. Bain accompanied his employer into the street, and stood on the pavement while Sir Aubrey mounted Splinter, whose sleek neck Mr. Bain patted approvingly.

' I wish I could get such a horse as that, Sir Aubrey; I'm generally pretty fortunate in horse-flesh, but I never met with anything to match him.'

Sir Aubrey smiled, and bent over Splinter affectionately.

' Six o'clock, Bain,' he said.

' Six o'clock, Sir Aubrey;' and Sir Aubrey shook his rein, and rode gaily down the High-street, pleased with the easy manner in which Shadrach Bain had taken the announcement of his marriage.

CHAPTER IV.

MR. BAIN went back to his office, seated himself at his desk, and gave himself up to deepest thought. It was not often that Mr. Bain thought. His active prosperous life was too busy to allow much margin for meditation. No twilight hour did Mr. Bain waste on those waking dreams in which some men let their fancies wander, pleased with shadows; nor did sad retrospective musings, tender memories of days that were gone, ever beguile Mr. Bain into forgetfulness of the present. He was a man who lived essentially in the life of to-day. The business in hand, however petty, was the supreme business of his existence. He brought all his forces into life's daily battle; and it was perhaps on this account that no one ever took him at a disadvantage.

But when Shadrach Bain did think, he thought

with all his might. See him now, elbows planted on his desk, chin set firmly on his clasped hands, and you see a man with whom thought is the impalpable scaffolding of a substantial edifice. The man does not think only—he builds. The constructive faculty—strongest organ in that strong brain—is hard at work. The closely knit brows denote that the architectural design in hand just now is complicated—there are difficulties even. For some time the thing seems impossible; then the keen eyes take a more resolute look, the firm lips tighten, and now relax into a slow smile. The difficulties are conquered, the airy scaffolding stands firm ; he sees it perfect in every angle, and the smile becomes almost triumphant. The plan of his future edifice is complete.

' Take thy bill and sit down quickly and write fifty,' repeated Mr. Bain, in a musing tone. ' I think I have made friends with the mammon of unrighteousness this morning.'

It was some time before Sir Aubrey's land steward settled to his daily work in his usual brisk manner. He opened a handsome japanned case on which were painted the magical words—Perriam Estate— and looked over a number of title-deeds. Some he threw on his left hand, and others on his right, until the parchments made two separate heaps.

On one of these he laid his hand firmly.

' All these my father and I added to the estate,' he said to himself. And it seemed to him that Sir Andrew and his son Sir Aubrey were as ciphers when weighed in the balance with his father and himself.

' Why not five thousand a year?' he mused. ' Why not seven? But no doubt Sir Aubrey will leave her all he has to leave if she behaves well to him. What could a weak little thing like that do to offend him—a parish schoolmaster's daughter? I saw her once standing at the gate of the schoolhouse garden—a slim, fair-haired girl, with brown eyes. Pretty enough, I daresay. But I was driving too fast to take much notice. A girl that could be moulded to anything, no doubt. There'll be a fine estate by the time she's a widow—a fine independent estate. And if the heir-at-law should turn me out of the old property I shall still have my grip upon Perriam.'

Rarely had Shadrach Bain spent so much time upon meditation—upon thought which soared out of the narrow circle of the present into the wide cloud-land of the future—as he spent this morning. He had no actual work, no file of sharp, short, decisive letters ready for the copying machine, to show for his departed morning when the brazen tongue of the family bell gave note of the one o'clock dinner. He started up from his chair with a surprised look, and made haste to wash his hands at the well-appointed lavatory in a little room beyond the clerks' office.

It was an established rule in Monkhampton—strict as Jewish law—that the middle classes, the simple respectable people, who prided themselves on their simplicity and respectability, should dine at one o'clock. However laggard appetite might be, the family board was spread with plain substantial fare at that particular hour. Families who hungered after fashion, or even what was called gentility, might dine later if they pleased—might have an untidy scrambling meal in the middle of the day called luncheon, and an early supper at seven—disguised under the name of dinner, and call that fashion. By so doing they cut themselves off from those prouder burghers who clung tenaciously to the manners and customs of their forefathers. Mr. Bain was of the old school, and, though there had been vague half-expressed aspirations on the part of his daughters for late dinners and equestrian exercise, those yearnings had been stifled in the birth.

Neither Matilda Jane nor Clara Louisa had dared to give them utterance in their father's hearing.

The dining-room—that apartment whose crimson moreen curtains were visible from the street—was a comfortable square room, with panelled walls, painted and grained, in the semblance of dark oak, and graced with family portraiture, in which the high waists and floral head-gear, the buff waistcoats, ponderous watch-chains, and formidable shirt frills of the George and William period were preserved in effigy for the gratification of posterity. The furniture was of the same era, and was as solid as it was ugly. The silver of the neatly laid dinner-table was of the Puritanic fiddle pattern ; the Delft dinner service was of honest willow—but a superior willow, relieved about the rims and handles of vegetable dishes and soup tureens with a little gilding. The damask napery was of spotless purity. Everything indicated that honest middle-class prosperity which follows not the changes of fashion—housekeeping which goes on to-day exactly as it was begun twenty years ago.

Had Mr. Bain been of an epicurean temper, he might have made some murmur against the placid monotony of his daily fare. The endless procession of legs of mutton and wing ribs of beef, varied occasionally by a roast of pork, a Sabbath fillet of veal, a

Michaelmas goose, a Saturday beef-steak pie. But, if not altogether an intellectual man, Mr. Bain was certainly not **a slave** to his senses, and provided he ate when **he was hungry cared but little** with what **viands he was fed.** The joint was well cooked and cleanly served, **the** potatoes were well boiled, and the cook had her gamut of substantial old English puddings with which to embellish the meal. Pud-**ding every other day** was the rule of the Bain house-**hold.** They **could quite** as well have afforded them-selves pudding every day, but Mrs. Bain, who looked at life from a pious standpoint, considered daily pudding a pampering of the flesh. There was always a blank look upon the faces of the younger members **on** off days, **and Mrs. Bain felt that those lenten** deprivations all the year round were a blessing to her offspring. A provident wife and a thoughtful mother of the old Puritan type this Mrs. Bain, and her husband felt **that in** Louisa Dawker he had secured **a treasure,** even putting her six thousand pounds out of the question. Unhappily, for the last three years, Mrs. Bain had been more or less of an invalid —obliged to wear a respirator all the winter—unable to go out of doors after sunset, even in summer, keeping her bed at times, and suffering much from complicated **ailments** of lungs and throat, which, as the family doctor had whispered, must some day prove fatal, but bearing up bravely through all, and keeping her husband's house vigilantly even when illness made her a prisoner in her bedroom. Summer was a kindly season for Mrs. Bain, and while the warm weather lasted she seemed tolerably brisk, and took her seat at the head of the table, and carved the joint for the seven healthy sons and daughters, Mr. Bain not caring to be troubled by the wants of these young ravens. He liked to review his morning's work and plan his afternoon's labours as he eat his dinner.

Mrs. Bain was a small pale woman, with an honest, intelligent face, and dark eyes that had a pleasant softness in them. She had never been pretty, and failing health had now set the stamp of decay on her pallid countenance; but she looked what she was—a good woman. Her children loved her, despite her somewhat Puritan rule, which exacted a good deal of self-denial from these young people, and her husband respected her.

To-day the head of the household ate with less than his usual healthy appetite. So languidly indeed did Mr. Bain ply his knife and fork as to draw upon himself the notice of his family.

' Aren't you well, father ? ' asked Matilda Jane,

the eldest daughter, 'you're hardly eating anything.'

'I hope the beef isn't too much done for you,
father,' said the house-mother with affectionate
solicitude. 'I always tells Betsy to do it with the
gravy in. And it's a very fine wing rib to-day. The
joint weighed fifteen pounds eleven ounces. I saw
it in the scale myself.'

'The beef's very good, mother, but I've not much
of an appetite, and this is only to be my luncheon.
I'm to dine with Sir Aubrey at seven.'

'Another lease, I suppose?'

'Something in that way,' replied Shadrach.

'I heard Sir Aubrey's horse stop before our door
while I was in the kitchen talking to cook,' said Mrs.
Bain, 'and I thought it must be something particular to bring him here so early.'

'It was some rather important business,' replied
the lawyer.

The family evinced no curiosity. Leases, and
small purchases of land, alterations, improvements,
drainage, waste bits of ground reclaimed, were not
subjects to engage the interest of the female mind.
Mr. Bain's sons were too young to sympathize with
his industry. Their minds were absorbed by football, cricket, and the fourth book of the Æneid.

No one questioned him further about Sir Aubrey's visit.

'You were at Hedingham Fancy Fair, you two girls, weren't you?' asked Mr. Bain presently.

'Yes, father,' replied the elder. 'Mrs. Thomas Toynbee asked us to go with her daughters. The Toynbees are Church of England people, you know, and Mr. Thomas Toynbee is first cousin to Mr. Toynbee of Hedingham, the rich manufacturer. Mother said we might go—she thought you wouldn't mind for once in a way, though they're not chapel people.'

'I've no objection,' said Mr. Bain. 'Did you see Miss—Miss Carew, I think it is—the schoolmaster's daughter, while you were there?'

'Yes, father. We went into the orchard to see the children at tea, and she was there.'

'A very pretty girl, isn't she?' inquired Mr. Bain.

His daughters looked at each other and deliberated.

'That's a matter of taste, father,' said Clara Louisa.

'She's not my style of beauty,' said Matilda Jane.

'But, I suppose, some people admire her,' added

Clara Louisa, 'for it is the common talk that Mr. Standen, of Dean House, is in love with her, and is most likely to marry her, if his mother doesn't interfere to prevent him.'

'Do you know anything about this Miss Carew? You've heard people talk about her, it seems. Have you ever heard what kind of a girl she is?'

'Lor, no, father; you don't suppose I know anybody who knows her? A parish schoolmaster's daughter! The Miss Toynbees of Hedingham teach in the Sunday-school sometimes, and they told their cousins that they considered Sylvia Carew excessively vain, and very much above her station in all her notions; a girl who wanted setting down. That's what the Miss Toynbees said.'

'Humph,' said Mr. Bain; 'that's what the Miss Toynbees said, is it?' And then within himself he reflected that perhaps it would be Sylvia's privilege to set down the Miss Toynbees, rather than to be set down by them.

Not a hint of Sir Aubrey's marriage did Shadrach Bain give to his family circle. Sir Aubrey had announced that event to him in the strictest confidence, and the agent showed himself worthy of the trust.

He was hardly up to his usual standard of mental activity all that afternoon. This business of Sir

Aubrey's marriage was too startling to be easily put out of his mind. He wrote letters, looked over the rent book, saw two or three Monkhampton clients, and got through his work tolerably well, but his mind was only half in it. He was glad when it was time to order the dog-cart for his drive to Perriam, glad to turn his back upon the common work of the office, and go up to his own room to dress.

He looked as good a gentleman as the best in Monkhampton when he came downstairs at a quarter-past five, clad in a suit of plainest black, with neat boots, slender watch-chain, faultless shirt-front of unadorned linen—clean—well brushed—a model country gentleman. Thus attired, his family looked up to him with reverential admiration.

'How well you would look in the pulpit, father, dressed like that!' said Matilda Jane.

Mr. Bain smiled as he adjusted his neckcloth before the looking-glass over the dining-room chimney-piece, while his admiring family sat round the table taking their tea.

'How much better I should look in the House of Commons,' he said to himself, not ill-pleased with his own image in the glass: 'and who knows what may happen, if I keep my grip upon the Perriam property?'

' Do you think you shall be late, Shadrach ?' asked Mrs. Bain meekly. There was no such thing as a latchkey in the Bain household. The head of the family was all sobriety and steadiness. But he was the undisputed master of his ways, and if he chose, for some wise purpose of his own, to stay out late nobody would question his right.

' No, my dear ; Sir Aubrey never sits up late, as you know.'

' I thought there might be a party, Shadrach.'

' Party ?' cried Mr. Bain, ' as if Sir Aubrey ever asked me to his parties, or ever gave any, for the matter of that. What could put such a notion into your head, Louisa ?'

' I don't know,' answered Mrs. Bain. ' You've dressed more particularly than usual. That's the last new suit Frazer sent you home, isn't it ? You said you shouldn't begin to wear it just yet.'

' The old one's an uncomfortable fit. Besides, what's the use of having good clothes lying hidden in a chest of drawers ? There's the trap ? Good-bye, Louisa ; good-bye, girls and boys.'

CHAPTER V.

THE dinner at Perriam Place was a very quiet business. Mr. Carew and his daughter found the drawing-room empty of human life when they entered it a few moments before seven. That vast apartment, with its massive but somewhat scanty furniture, had a melancholy look in the evening light. The size and grandeur of the room seemed to cry aloud for people to inhabit it. Mr. Carew, who, like all self-indulgent people, was easily affected by external influences, gave a faint shudder as his gaze wandered round the spacious, lofty saloon.

'A fine room,' he said, 'but rather dismal.' Sylvia looked about her curiously. She was glad of the opportunity to examine these splendours. On her previous visit the room had been at first half in shadow, and then but dimly lighted by solitary lamps and candles, and the master of the house had been present. Any inspection of the apartment had been therefore impossible. To-day she was able to take a deliberate survey—and to-day she contemplated the room with a new feeling. A month hence it would be her very own. She walked slowly up and down, looking at the tall china jars, the wire-guarded bookcases, the massive sofas, the bare tables.

'What curious foreign-looking curtains!' she exclaimed, examining the Oriental embroidery. 'But they are a good deal faded. I think I shall persuade Sir Aubrey to have new ones—amber satin would be the thing for this room.'

'I hope you will find Sir Aubrey compliant enough to oblige you,' answered her father, remembering that interview of last night, in which the baronet had appeared to him by no means pliant.

'Oh, I am not afraid of that,' returned Sylvia, smiling at her own image in the tall narrow glass between the windows. 'And when I am Lady Perriam'—she never said 'when I am married,' but always 'when I am Lady Perriam'—'I shall give large parties, and this room will look as it ought to look. It's a superb room for parties, isn't it, papa?'

'No doubt. But I don't fancy Sir Aubrey is a

party-giving man. People have talked a good deal about his keeping himself shut up here and hardly seeing anybody.'

'How can you be so stupid, papa? Of course as a bachelor Sir Aubrey would care very little for company. But it will be different when he is married. Do you suppose I mean to be buried alive when I am Lady Perriam? It would be much better for me to marry Edmund if there were any chance of that.'

'Of course not, my love,' replied her father hastily. 'Pray don't talk of young Standen. It is treason against Sir Aubrey to remember his insignificant existence.'

Sylvia sighed. The mere mention of her first lover's name brought a flood of sad memories—memories that were sweet as well as sad. She thought of the summer evenings they had spent together a little while ago. A little while! It seemed now as if she were divided from that too recent past by the space of half a lifetime.

'I feel ten years older since I accepted Sir Aubrey,' she thought, with another sigh.

The inspection of the saloon had no further charm for her. She flung herself into a chair by an open window, and sat there silent, dejected. Her father looked at her with some concern ; not for his daughter's feelings, but for his own chances of that promised hundred per annum.

'If you are going to give yourself sentimental airs about Edmund Standen, the sooner you tell Sir Aubrey the state of the case and give up the notion of being Lady Perriam the better,' said the schoolmaster sternly. He felt that it was no time for soft pleading.

Before Sylvia could answer him the door opened, and Sir Aubrey came in, followed by his land steward.

The baronet crossed the room to greet his betrothed. Mr. Bain walked towards the empty fireplace, at which Mr. Carew had taken his stand.

'My dear Sylvia, I owe you a hundred apologies,' said the baronet, after pressing the hand which was somewhat coldly offered to him. 'I have been detained, talking to Bain, my lawyer and agent; but as our conversation concerned your future interests I hope you will forgive me.'

'There is nothing to forgive, Sir Aubrey,' answered Sylvia, and then in a lower voice she added, 'I have to thank you for your kindness in giving papa the money for my *trousseau*. I know it is not customary, but we are such paupers—and I cannot refuse your gift.'

Tears, the tears of wounded pride, were in her eyes as she spoke. She had heard so much about *trousseaux* from Mary Peter, and she knew that it was always the bride's father who provided his daughter's outfit. Hers seemed almost the gift of charity.

'My dearest, pray do not mention such a trifle. I hope you had a pleasant drive here.'

'Very pleasant. How thoughtful it was of you to send the carriage!'

'It will be your own carriage very soon, to order whenever you like.'

That was a consoling thought. Those proud tears were quickly dried.

It would be very nice to spend Sir Aubrey's hundred pounds too, although it had been a somewhat humiliating business to accept it. Sylvia meant to devote the next day to shopping. What delight to walk into Ganzlein's and feel that she could buy whatever she pleased! She could not imagine her fancies soaring beyond the limit of a hundred pounds.

'By-the-bye,' said Sir Aubrey, when they had talked a little about the weather, and about Perriam, which the baronet liked to hear praised, 'I must introduce my agent, Mr. Bain. A very useful

and estimable person. He takes the entire management of my estate, takes all trouble off my hands;
so that I have nothing to do except receive my
rents. Come here, Bain, I want to present you to
Miss Carew.'

Mr. Bain obeyed the summons. He had seen the
slim white-robed figure from a distance, and his
keen eye had taken in every detail of that graceful
form. But Sylvia's face had been turned away from
him, and he saw it now for the first time, in the
clear soft light of the summer evening.

He bowed, murmured something indistinct about
the honour he derived from the introduction, and
then stood silently awaiting his patron's next address.
He looked at Sylvia, but that steadfast straight-
forward look of his told nothing of the man's
thoughts.

He was thinking that this girl was lovely enough
to bewitch a wiser man than Sir Aubrey Perriam,
thinking even that he, Shadrack Bain, had never
seen real beauty until to-night, that all the pretty
young women it had been his advantage to behold at
divers periods of his existence had been but as
images of clay compared to this perfect and delicate porcelain. This pale, blossom-like loveliness
was a style of beauty he had never met with. Those

deeply lustrous hazel eyes were as strange to him as the flora in some newly discovered island of the Pacific is strange to the botanist.

But Shadrack Bain was not a man to be deeply moved by beauty, however unfamiliar. He wondered and he admired, but no flutter of his strong heart paid tribute to Sylvia's power to charm. Had she been his own daughter he could have hardly contemplated her with a more calmly critical eye.

He was, however, essentially a practical man—a man who looked at everybody from one point of view, and measured everything by one standard. That standard was self-interest. In his prolonged meditations he had made up his mind that Sylvia must come into the scheme of his life. She might be fit or unfit to fill that square in the geometrical plan of his destiny which he intended her to fill, but if unfit she must be made fit. Upon that point Mr. Bain had no doubt.

Mr. Perriam shuffled into the room presently in his old-fashioned dress-coat, and short black trousers of antique cut, and white stockings and ancient shoes, with loosely tied ribbons, looking like an elderly copy of his brother indifferently executed. It was a singular evidence of the unwholesomeness of a sedentary and secluded life that Mordred Perriam looked ten years older than his elder and more active brother.

The butler announced dinner, and they went to the dining-room, Sylvia on Sir Aubrey's arm, Mordred and Mr. Carew side by side, talking of books— or rather Mordred talking and the schoolmaster pretending to be interested—Shadrack Bain stalking behind them, silent and alone. The butler planted them out at the long table, far apart, like young trees on a new estate ; so remote from one another that conversation had a forced air. It was like hailing to somebody on the opposite side of a street. Sylvia sat next Sir Aubrey, and as the dinner proceeded he contrived to draw his chair a little nearer hers, so that their talk should be unheard by the rest. Mr. Bain ate his dinner in almost absolute silence. Like a guest at a royal table, he waited to be spoken to ; and as no one spoke to him he remained discreetly mute. Mordred twaddled on unendingly to Mr. Carew. Sir Aubrey devoted himself exclusively to his future bride. But Mr. Bain ate his dinner and amused himself with his own thoughts, and wore the aspect of a contented mind. Now and then he stole a little look at Sylvia ; once or twice he smiled to himself—a slow, thoughtful smile—and that was all.

The meal itself was good and ample, but scrupulously simple—a dinner of the old-fashioned, substantial order, not nearly so grand as the dinners given by Mrs. Toynbee, which Sylvia had heard described by Mary Peter, the village gossip—dinners which were in preparation for days before the festival, and at which Monkhampton confectioners came to assist.

Sylvia admired the handsome old china, with its dark reds and deep purples and rich gilding—the massive old-fashioned silver, a trifle clumsy, perhaps, but with such a look of long-established wealth and state. The room in which they dined was sombre, but its very gloom had an air of grandeur. The voluminous curtains of darkest crimson velvet were in perfect tone with the oak panelling; the wide mantelpiece of dark green marble was supported upon clustered columns of white veinless stone, with bases and capitals of red porphyry. This, the handsomest object in the room, relieved the darker hues of the walls and furniture.

The gentlemen, at Sir Aubrey's suggestion, returned to the drawing-room with Sylvia, and then followed one of those evenings which irreverent minds distinguish as ' slow.' Sir Aubrey naturally devoted himself to his betrothed. He showed her the various but not numerous objects of interest in the saloon; told her the history of each. How those vases had been sent from India by a certain General Perriam, his Great Uncle; how those curtains had been worked by Hindoos who squatted on the floor of the corridor outside his Great Aunt's apartments in Calcutta, and who were paid so many pice a day for their labours. He took Sylvia to the library, and showed her that apartment, a treasury of learning which hardly wore the most attractive shape. Here, indeed, the severer muses seemed to frown forbiddingly upon the young student. The lightest book on yonder massive carved oak shelves was Spenser's Fairy Queen, and even that work of fancy was rendered outwardly repulsive by its dingy binding.

Sir Aubrey showed Sylvia the table at which he was wont to write letters and transact his business with Mr. Bain—an old office desk, covered with well worn leather.

'The library is not so pretty as the drawing-room,' said Sylvia.

'No,' replied the baronet, 'a library is for use. One does not expect prettiness in a library.'

'Are the books very nice?' Sylvia asked timidly. It was too dark for her to read the titles, and she thought those dingy volumes might possibly belie their outward show.

'Well, I don't quite know a young lady's idea of niceness in books. You like the Sorrows of Werter, by the way, a flimsy, sentimental piece of nonsense, which took the world by storm in my father's time. There's nothing here of the Werter kind—in point of fact, no works of fiction. There's a fine edition of Holinshed yonder, Froissart's Chronicles, the Mort d'Arthur; sermons, from Latimer down to South and Barrow; Milton's Prose Works; Rollin, Hume, and all the best historians.'

'Macaulay and Carlyle?' asked Sylvia, thinking there might be something readable in that way. She liked history as interpreted by these brilliant and diverse pens.

'No. There has been nothing added within the last fifty years. It was my grandfather who completed the library.'

'As if a library could ever be complete,' thought Sylvia.

It was pleasant to imagine the changes she would make in this gloomy temple of the learned dead. New curtains of bright glowing hue, instead of that black-green velvet, which age and dust had darkened to the colour of the trunks of moss-grown trees; a new carpet to replace that worn and faded Turkey, where every shade had worn to one neutrality of tint; new tables; stands for engravings; new chairs — roomy, luxurious, covered with crimson morocco, and decorated with crest and monogram in gold. She had seen the luxuries of life, were it but in the upholsterer's window at Monkhampton.

They went back to the saloon, after making the circuit of the lower rooms, the hall, the music-room, long disused, a spacious empty chamber whose walls gave back sonorous echoes, the breakfast-parlour, the late Lady Perriam's morning-room.

'I'll show you my brother's rooms another day,' said Sir Aubrey. 'They are on the upper floor. There's not much to admire in them except the number of his books.'

In the saloon they found Mr. Carew yawning over his empty teacup; Mordred furtively devouring the catalogue of a forthcoming auction in last Saturday's *Athenæum;* Mr. Bain meditative—altogther a silent party.

'You seem rather dull,' said the baronet blandly. 'I must get a piano by-and-by. It's a pity we haven't one, for Miss Carew might have given us some music.'

Miss Carew looked about the room, and thought

how many things it wanted besides a piano to make
it thoroughly pleasant.   That grand old-world air
was very well in its way, but Sylvia longed for
modern luxury as well as antique stateliness.   It
was agreeable to contemplate an apartment which
reminded one of the 'Spectator,' and Pope's
Belinda; but one could not quite ignore the
strides which modern invention had made in the
art of comfort.

It was a long evening.   Devoted as Sir Aubrey
was, he had not very much to say to his betrothed.
The eyes which delighted him inspired no eloquence
of speech.   What he did say to her was chiefly
about himself.   Of books he knew little, save the
works of Addison, Pope, Swift, Voltaire, and a few
more of the same period.   Of men he knew still
less.   So he told Sylvia mild little anecdotes of his
blameless youth, his revered mother, his admirable
father, and now and then brought forth some inane
little joke which had been handed down from father
to son like an heirloom.

Sylvia listened—smiled even at the jokelets—
but thought with a bitter pang of Edmund's swift
flowing talk—a good deal of it nonsense, perhaps,
but always eloquent nonsense—talk about poets,
playwrights, romancers; talk which sparkled often

with the brightness of ideas which were not all borrowed; talk which was vigorous with the force and passion of youth.

'I shall never hear him again. I shall never walk with him in the dear old lanes at sunset,' she said to herself. 'But then I shall be Lady Perriam. I shall be mistress of this grand old house.'

Splendid as Perriam Place might be, its future mistress was very glad to get away from it on this particular evening. She gave a sigh of relief as the carriage door was shut, and the slow, steady old horses began their jog-trot progress.

'Sir Aubrey is very kind, papa,' she said, as if apologizing for the sigh; 'but rather dull. At least he was rather dull to-night.'

'Not half so dull as his brother. I've been bored to death by those tedious stories about second-hand books. I thought you seemed very well amused with Sir Aubrey. I heard you laugh ever so many times.'

'One is obliged to laugh when people tell one anecdotes. But that kind of laughter is very fatiguing. I feel as tired as if I'd been teaching all day in the Sunday-school. I wonder whether good society is always fatiguing?'

Mr. Carew did not answer this speculative inquiry. He remembered society that had known no weariness. Those snug little dinners in the Kilburn villa—those gay summer evenings in the shrubberied garden, when he and his guests took their coffee outside the jasmine-shrouded verandah, by the light of the midsummer stars; that inexhaustible talk of men and horses, and art and music; and for the centre of the picture the fair face of his pretty wife, the cynosure of all other eyes, if not his own lode-star. This society, for which James Carew had sacrificed honour and honesty, if not altogether 'good,' had at least never been dull.

Sylvia nestled into the padded corner of the comfortable old carriage, and thought of her shopping at Monkhampton to-morrow. She had taken the bank-notes from her father, and had reluctantly relinquished one ten-pound note to that parent when he pleaded his poverty and embarrassments.

'A hundred pounds is not much towards such a *trousseau* as I ought to have, papa,' she had said somewhat dolefully. 'It seems rather hard that you should want to take any of it away.'

'It seems harder that you should grudge your father a trifle out of such a windfall,' answered the schoolmaster bitterly. 'What do you want with a heap of fine clothes? Sir Aubrey will give you anything you ask him for when you are his wife.'

There was that other claimant, the wretched woman in Bell-alley, Fetter-lane. Sylvia did not quite forget that still stronger call upon a daughter's benevolence.

'I'll send her five pounds from Monkhampton to-morrow,' she said to herself. 'When I am Lady Perriam I can often send her money.'

*   *   *   *   *   *

Before starting for Monkhampton Sylvia took Mary Peter, the dressmaker, in some measure into her confidence. She told this useful friend of her speedy marriage, but as she said nothing about the bridegroom Miss Peter naturally concluded that Edmund Standen was that happy man. Sylvia wanted the dressmaker's aid in the choice of fabrics, the adjustment of quantities, and there was a pleasant sensation in going to Monkhampton in the fly from the inn, attended by Mary Peter. The driving from shop to shop was like a triumphal progress, and it was a new rapture to be able to choose the prettiest things—those perfect boots which Sylvia had gazed at with envious sighs in the leading bootmaker's neatly arranged window—the lustrous silks, the soft lace, the delicate embroidery. Sylvia was surprised to find how speedily her bank-notes melted away when she chose the best and choicest articles in Mr. Ganzlein's emporium. Mary Peter kept whispering to her that she must have twenty yards of this, and seventeen of that, and ten yards of the broad Brussels lace for a trimming, and three or four pieces of Madeira work for the under linen which Miss Peter was to put in hand for her. She found that seventy pounds was a mere nothing to spend at Mr. Ganzlein's, and that she must restrict her purchases to three or four dresses at the most.

That thick corded silk of pearliest white which she selected, after much deliberation, for the wedding dress, would do for a dinner dress afterwards, Mary told her, and would dye after that.

'Dye,' exclaimed Sylvia, forgetting her previous reticence, 'do you suppose I shall ever wear dyed silks?'

'Well, I don't know why you shouldn't, Sylvia. Rich people wear them. I made up a dyed moire antique for Mrs. Toynbee last spring, and it looked very rich, but was just a little streaky by daylight. You might have your wedding dress dyed a lovely blue next year.'

Sylvia chose a dove-coloured silk—the real dove-colour—and a delicate gray. She remembered Sir

Aubrey's charge about simplicity, and she fancied these subdued tints could scarcely fail to please him. She bought a good deal of lace, some linen fine enough for a Princess of the blood Royal, a morning dress or two of plain white cambric, a black silk mantle, and a warm shawl for travelling, and found that these purchases absorbed the whole of her seventy pounds. Ten more pounds were expended at the fashionable bootmaker's aforementioned, and at the chief perfumer and hairdresser's establishment, where Sylvia chose brushes and combs fit for the future Lady Perriam.

'I haven't even money enough left for a dressing bag,' said Sylvia dolefully, when she looked into her almost empty purse, which had seemed full to plethora a little while ago.

'I dare say Mr. Standen will give you one,' returned Miss Peter; 'they generally do.' *They* meaning the hapless bridegroom species.

Sylvia gave a little start at the sound of that too familiar name. The thought of Edmund would come ever and anon to dash her sense of triumph, nay, to make all things bitterness to her.

The two young women drove home merrily enough notwithstanding. They discussed the making of the dresses, and Sylvia gave her orders with the air of an empress. She begged that Mary would be very particular as to the neatness of the work, and desired that the style should be elegantly simple. There were to be none of the frillings, and crossway bands, and puffings, and fringes, and tassels, and gimps which Mrs. Toynbee delighted in. 'I can afford to dispense with trimming,' Sylvia remarked grandly.

'You will put off all other work, of course, for a wedding order,' she said to her satellite at parting; 'but, remember, you must tell no one whose wedding dresses you are making. I don't want people to know anything about my marriage till it's over!'

'I suppose it's to be directly he comes back from Demerara?' hazarded Mary.

'Never mind when it is to be. Mind I want my dresses in three weeks from to-day.'

'I believe it's a moriel impossible,' answered Mary, who had vague ideas about certain substantives, and said impossible for impossibility; 'but if it's in human nature to get through so much work in that time I'll do it.'

Sylvia thought of the dressmaker's bill. She had but one ten-pound note left, and five pounds out of that she had intended for her mother; but she now decided on keeping the money for Mary Peter. It would not do to enter her new stage of existence in debt to a village dressmaker. She would send Mrs. Carford money after her marriage.

Thus it happened that the lodger in Bell-alley profited nothing by Sir Aubrey's hundred pounds.

Before nightfall a great many people in Monk-hampton had heard of Miss Carew's purchases at Ganzlein's. The schoolmaster's daughter was very well known in the shop, though her outlay heretofore had been most meagre—a yard or two of ribbon, a cheap muslin dress, a pair of gloves, and so on. That expenditure of seventy pounds had made the grave Ganzlein himself open his eyes to the widest extent as he stood at his desk in a dark corner of the shop, counting out Miss Carew's money. He talked of the circumstance at dinner in the bosom of his family, opining that her marriage with Edmund Standen was to take place very soon; and there was a good deal said by Mrs. and the Miss Ganzleins about Mr. Standen's foolish infatuation.

'Young Standen must have given her the money she laid out to-day,' observed the draper. 'She couldn't have got it from her father.'

'Everybody's mad about that girl, I think,' returned Mrs. Ganzlein. 'I was told only yesterday that Sir Aubrey had taken notice of her and her father, and had them up at the Place.'

CHAPTER VI.

THE swift days went past. Very swift they seemed to Sylvia, and yet very slow. She had chosen her own fate, yet she felt in a manner doomed. There were times when she felt as helpless as the luckless sailor clasped in the pulpy embrace of that sea-monster whose gelatinous arms are stretched out of the sea to draw the victim to his death. The sea-monster was Fate.

The letter to Demerara was gone now; it was hastening over the wide blue sea. How happy Sylvia would have been had she been sailing over the wide ocean, instead of that false, deceitful letter, the letter in which she surrendered her love, with tears, for his own sake.

He would return—too soon, come when he would —to find her another man's wife. O! bitter awakening from his brief dream of woman's fidelity!

Sylvia paid no more visits to Perriam Place during the brief period of her betrothal. Sir Aubrey would have liked her to be there often, but many such visits would have set people talking; and he wanted to stave off all gossip and wonderment till after his marriage. He made all the necessary arrangements as secretly as if he had been chief conspirator in a new gunpowder plot; procured the licence; and executed that deed of settlement one morning in Mr. Bain's office, where Sylvia, in her white bonnet and pale muslin dress, looked like a hothouse plant that some wind had blown there.

The days went by, the long summer evenings dwindled. The July moon shrank and waned, August was very near. Then came the first week of August. The reapers were abroad in the land. The frightened corncrake knew not whither to betake himself. The heavy wains rolled homeward in the shortening twilight. Sylvia's wedding day was at hand.

Sir Aubrey spent all his evenings in the school-house parlour, which was perhaps a more cheerful apartment for the occupation of three people than that too spacious saloon at Perriam. He came under cover of dusk for the most part, being so anxious to preserve the secret of his wooing—came

to sit opposite his betrothed, while she beguiled the
evening with some trifling fancy work, and to discourse mildly, as he had discoursed at Perriam,
repeating himself a little now and then. He was
rather fond of talking politics, and as his opinions
were of the good old Tory school, hardly modified
since the days of Chatham and North, and Mr.
Carew, like most disappointed men, was a virulent
Radical, there was plenty of room for argument
between these two politicians. Sylvia wondered that
people could talk so much and get so angry about
things which seemed really to matter very little to
anybody outside the House of Commons. The world
seemed to go on pretty much the same whether
Conservatives or Liberals were dominant, and rates
and taxes were just as hard to pay whether one
Chancellor of the Exchequer or another dipped his
fingers into the purses of the people.

Mary Peter brought the dresses home one by one,
and their simple magnificence almost astonished the
enraptured possessor.

'I think that's heavenly,' exclaimed Mary, as she
held up the dove-coloured silk in the little cottage
bed-chamber, and shook out its lustrous folds with
the mantua-maker's skilled hand. 'It pays you well,
Sylvia, though you did give ten and six a yard for it.

I haven't made up many richer silks, not even for Mrs. Standen—your mother-in-law that is to be,' added Mary jocosely.

There was hardly room for all the finery in Sylvia's small bedroom.   Her riches were almost embarrassing.   The dresses lay about covered with clean linen, like bodies laid out in a hospital.

'You've got new trunks to put them in, I hope,' said Mary. 'There's nothing I like to see better than handsome portmanteaux, when a bride's going off for the wedding trip.'

Sylvia sighed despairingly.

'I haven't a box belonging to me,' she said ; 'I've never travelled anywhere like other people.'

'Then, I daresay Mr. Standen will give you a couple of handsome trunks.   You've only to drop an 'int when he comes back.'

'I hate hints,' returned Sylvia ; 'I must ask him to give me some boxes.'

She made the request to Sir Aubrey that evening, when he inquired if she were nearly ready for the wedding journey—only three days now remained before the appointed date.   Mr. Vancourt, the vicar, had received notice of the marriage—all arrangements were made.

'My dresses are quite ready, Sir Aubrey,'

she replied, 'but I have no boxes to put them in.'

'You'd better order a couple of fair-sized portmanteaux at Folthorpe's. Don't have them too large, they're a nuisance in travelling, and the French railways charge for all luggage.'

'I am sorry that I spent all my money before I thought of the trunks,' said Sylvia, blushing deeply. It was hard to beg, even of her betrothed, though she thought of him in the future as a person who would give her everything she desired, whose purse she could draw upon with perfect freedom.

Sir Aubrey stared at her somewhat blankly.

'Oh, you have spent that hundred pounds,' he said, taken off his guard by an announcement which considerably surprised him, in his happy ignorance of feminine costliness. 'I fear you've been buying a good deal of unnecessary finery.'

'I hope not, Sir Aubrey. I have tried to choose things to please you,' the girl answered quickly, tears of humiliation starting in her eyes.

'My dearest, pray don't think that I am vexed with you,' cried the baronet, melted by that tearful look in those lovely eyes. 'The money was yours to do what you liked with. I'll order your portmanteaux to-morrow morning.'

He had as yet given her but one present besides that utilitarian offering of bank-notes. His single gift was an old-fashioned diamond hoop ring of his mother's; the diamonds set in time-darkened silver, and encircling the finger. This was doubtless but an earnest of the splendours which he would heap upon her by-and-by.

The wedding day arrived—a misty August morning; the hills and woods around Hedingham were shrouded in light summer vapour, which melted slowly before the sun. Sylvia heard the cheery voices of the reapers in the barley field yonder, and envied them their careless liberty. They were not going to be married. It was not the most awful day in their lives. They were not going to set a solemn seal upon their destinies, binding them to an unknown master for all time to come.

Only on the very threshold of doom did Sylvia pause to consider what she was doing. She dressed herself in the white silk wedding gown, unassisted, and wondered a little at her own beauty as she saw herself in the glass. That shining, pearly fabric, so trying to lesser loveliness, became her as its petals become the lily. But at this last moment she felt that her wedding dress was too fine for her wedding. There were to be no bridesmaids, no guests, no breakfast. She was to walk from the garden to the church on her father's arm, unseen, unadmired, to meet Sir Aubrey and Mr. Bain in the vestry, and directly the ceremony was over she was to put on her travelling dress and drive off to Monkhampton station with her elderly husband. It was not such a wedding as her dreams had shadowed forth when she was betrothed to Edmund Standen. In those vague, girlish visions she had pictured her wedding all gaiety and brightness, her village friends looking on admiringly, the school-children strewing her path with flowers.

'This lovely dress is quite thrown away,' she thought, with a discontented sigh. 'No one will see it but papa, and Sir Aubrey and Mr. Bain. I might just as well have kept the money it cost; only it would seem so strange to be married in colours.'

Her father made some remarks of a disparaging kind when she went downstairs in her radiant toilet.

'You'd better have been married in your travelling dress,' he said; 'that white thing's quite out of place for a private wedding. Sir Aubrey wanted to drive straight off from the churchyard gate.'

Sylvia pouted, and reflected with some self-gratulation that her father would hardly presume to question her actions when she was Lady Perriam.

' I shan't be ten minutes changing my dress,' she answered. ' Sir Aubrey must wait.'

' Must wait, must he? These are early days to talk of must.'

' Do you think I am going to be dictated to like a little child when I am married? ' Sylvia asked haughtily.

' I think you will have to behave a little more amiably to Sir Aubrey than you have behaved to me,' answered her father.

' I shall not have to cook his dinners at any rate,' retorted Sylvia. And in this Christian frame of mind father and daughter repaired, arm in arm, to the parish church.

Sir Aubrey and Mr. Bain were on the ground before them. The bridegroom gave a little start at sight of the bride's white robes. He had expected to see her dressed ready for their journey; but he could not complain when she looked so lovely. He uttered an admiring exclamation, and raised her hand to his lips with that stately gallantry which so well became him. Mr. Vancourt was ready for them, and his countenance gave no indication of the surprise which must have reigned within him at this

singular union. He performed the ceremony with
an agreeable briskness, and Sir Aubrey found himself a married man sooner than he could have
believed possible.

Mr. Bain was very attentive to the ceremony, and
curiously watchful of the bride, in his quiet way.
Sylvia's manner was emotionless in the extreme;
emotionless almost to apathy. There are awful
moments in life when the feelings seem be-
numbed. Sylvia felt nothing but a vague sense
of wonder. How had this thing come to pass so
speedily?

'Let me be the first to salute Lady Perriam,'
said Mr. Bain, when they had signed the register
in the vestry; and before any one could pro-
test against such an enormity, he had pressed
his lips upon Sylvia's fair forehead, the first kiss
that had rested there since Edmund's despairing
farewell. The bride drew back indignant at the
affront.

'It is the privilege of a best man,' apologized Mr.
Bain. 'Pray pardon me for having taken so great
a liberty, Lady Perriam.'

'Yes, my love,' said Sir Aubrey, putting aside the
absurdity of the business with an easy laugh; 'it
is Bain's privilege, I believe. You mustn't be angry

with him. But he might have waited for the second place.' And Sir Aubrey set the husband's first kiss on the lips of the bride. It seemed a preposterous thing that another man—his lawyer and steward—should have kissed her first.

CHAPTER VII.

' PASSION'S PASSING BELL.'

EDMUND STANDEN had been nearly three weeks in
Demerara, and had transacted the greater part of
the business that was required to be done in the
settlement of the late Mr. Sargent's affairs, when
the English mail brought him Sylvia's letter—the
letter of renunciation.

He sat for some minutes after he had finished
reading it, stupefied. It seemed like a bad dream.
That she, Sylvia Carew, who had laid her head upon
his breast in that fond farewell, and promised to be
faithful—that she could thus deliberately renounce
him, seemed a thing impossible of belief.

He read the letter slowly, thoughtfully, his senses
coming back to him by degrees. No, it was not a
jest, not a sportive girl's playful trifling with her
lover. It had been written in sober earnest. It was
a thoughtful, deliberate letter—logical even,—and
giving sound reasons for the writer's decision.

' She has grown very wise,' he said to himself bitterly, and then read the letter for a third time.

Love had such potent dominion over him that he could not long feel bitterly towards the writer of that miserable letter. The third perusal let in a new light upon the lines. This foolish epistle, which had given him so keen a pang, was but a proof of his darling's unselfishness—it showed him the noble mind of her he loved. For his own sake, out of concern for his welfare, she renounced him.

She preferred to remain in her obscure position, to endure her joyless life, rather than to accept the chances of his future; simply because she would not have him forfeit fortune for her sake. The letter breathed regretful love; her heart overflowed with tenderness for the man whose affection she renounced.

' Foolish child,' murmured Edmund, with a fond smile, ' more than foolish to think I would sacrifice her love for anything fortune can bestow. How could she have wavered so soon after our mutual vows of fidelity, when she knew that there was nothing but hopefulness in my mind. Can my mother have influenced her to write this letter? It looks rather like it. But, no, that's not possible.

My mother is incapable of falsehood or meanness. She promised to be kind to my darling while I was away. She would never take advantage of my absence to persuade Sylvia to renounce me.'

Whatever influence might have caused the writing of that letter, Mr. Standen had but one thought after receiving it, and that was an eager desire to get back to England as soon as it was practicable for him to return there. He completed the remainder of the business in hand, doing it well, though quickly. He persuaded Mrs. Sargent that for her own health and her children's an immediate departure was advisable, and prevailed upon the stricken widow to make herself and belongings ready to start by the next inter-colonial steamer to St. Thomas. Poor Mrs. Sargent obeyed her brother willingly enough. Had he not come to her as a protecting angel in the hour of her bitterest need? She was glad to leave the scenes where all her happiness was associated with the dead. The little black-frocked children were rejoiced to go to England in the big steamer, and talked rapturously of seeing grandmamma, whom the eldest could just remember. Edmund dilated on the delights of the Dean House gardens, and the English fruits and flowers, which were so different from the guava, tamarinds, plantains, and pine-apples familiar to these small colonists.

The duty of consoling his sister and amusing her children kept Edmund Standen too constantly engaged for much indulgence in morbid thoughts. The widowed voyager was ill and broken-spirited, and her brother had hard work to cheer her, were it ever so little. The small nephew and nieces were exacting. Edmund had actually no time for gloomy forebodings, which are generally the growth of leisure. He grew to think of the letter quite lightly. 'Dear foolish Sylvia, how could she suppose I would give her up?' he said to himself.

Although duty kept him closely employed, it could not altogether stifle impatience, and the voyage seemed longer than it would have appeared to a contented mind. He so longed to see his darling again, to gaze once more into the darkly luminous eyes and read there the tender denial of that foolish letter. When at last the steam wheels turned gaily in English waters, and the pretty Wight, clad in autumn's russet and gold, stole up out of the blue, his heart beat loud with joy. Southampton, commonplace enough to the common traveller, to the lover seemed a fairy city, whose pavements were golden.

Mr. Standen allowed the widow and orphans but

one night's rest at the Dolphin, ere he whisked them off to Monkhampton by the South-Western Railway. It was a long day's journey, with some changing of trains, and much delay at the junctions where they changed, and again uncle Edmund was fully employed by the claims of the widow and the small children. He was tired when they arrived at Monkhampton, where his mother's roomy landau and a cart for the luggage were in attendance. Edmund felt somewhat surprised that neither Mrs. Standen nor Esther had come to meet the travellers.

It was late in October, and, even in this genial climate, autumn's decaying touch had made havoc. The woods were lovely with that splendour which is the forerunner of death. The bare fields and busy plough spoke of seedtime and winter. The carriage wheels went silently over fallen leaves that lay deep in the unfrequented roads. How welcome was that simple beauty of English landscape to Edmund after the more lavish nature of South America!

He uttered that favourite exclamation of Englishmen:

'After all, there is no place like dear old England.' And England held Sylvia, that one lodestar of his soul.

Mrs. Sargent sighed plaintively.

' How happy I should be to return if I were coming back with George,' she murmured.

The children were gay enough, craning their young necks in all directions, struggling out of their nurse's arms, pointing to every dwelling they beheld, near or distant, and asking if that was grandmamma's house. Finding by degrees that a great many houses did not belong to grandmamma, they began to have a diminished idea of that lady's possessions.

But they came to Dean House at last: the staid, sober, old mansion, fronting the high road so boldly, and not pretending to be anything better than it was. There was the familiar iron gate, there the green tubs of scarlet geranium, still flourishing with luxuriant bloom. Edmund gave a little impatient sigh as he thought how much greeting he would have to go through, and how many maternal questions, fond and anxious, he would have to answer, before he could hurry off to Hedingham and clasp Sylvia to his breast. It would be night ere he crossed the old churchyard and opened the little gate into the schoolhouse garden, and saw the lighted windows of Sylvia's parlour. He could fancy her glad look of surprise when she opened the door in answer to his summons and saw him standing before her in the moonlight. Come back from the other side of the world, as it were; come back to claim her in spite of her letter.

The neat parlour-maid opened the glass door. The gardener and his underling came out to assist with the luggage; and while Edmund was lifting the children out of the carriage his mother appeared on the threshold with Esther Rochdale at her side.

The first glance told Edmund that their faces were not cheerful. It was in honour of George Sargent, of course, that they put on those sombre looks.

'It's a pity they should look so doleful,' thought Edmund. 'I've had sadness enough from Ellen all the way from Demerara, and now they remind her of her misfortunes instead of trying to make her forget them.'

He kissed his mother, who received him with deepest tenderness. 'My own brave son,' she said. 'Thank God for having brought you back to me.'

'How is Sylvia?' he asked eagerly. They were a little way apart from the widow, nurse, and children. The little ones were being kissed and welcomed by Esther Rochdale. She was delighted with these new claimants for her affections. Her happy, loving nature overflowed in fond caresses and pretty girlish talk.

'It does seem sweet to come to you,' said poor Ellen, and then melted to tears at the thought that she came without that other half of her own being, the idolized husband.

Edmund repeated his impatient question. His mother was slow to answer, but hung upon him with half-despairing fondness, as if he were going to be led off to execution in a minute or two.

'I don't know,' faltered Mrs. Standen. 'She is very well, I believe. I have not seen her lately. Come to your room, Edmund; you must be so tired. Change your dusty clothes, and come down to dinner. It has been ready for the last half-hour.'

'You haven't seen her lately!' repeated Edmund, ignoring Mrs. Standen's maternal solicitude. 'You promised you would be kind to her, mother.'

'Edmund,' said Mrs. Standen, with that steady, resolute look which her son knew so well, 'I will not say a word about Sylvia Carew till you have dined and rested a little.'

'Then I shall go to Hedingham this moment,' cried Edmund, snatching his hat from the slab where he had just now put it down.

'What, run away from your mother in the first

hour of your return to her? I am sorry you have no better idea of a son's duty.'

Edmund put his hat down again.

'You are too hard upon me, mother,' he said, melted, but yet reproachful. 'You don't consider how my heart yearns for her. I have had but one letter from her during my absence, and that a letter calculated to make me uncomfortable. I am dying to see her. But if you wish it I'll dine first. Only you might gratify me by speaking of her. Tell me that she is well and happy. That will last till I have dined, and can get to the dear old school-house.'

'I have every reason to believe that she is well and—prosperous.'

'Meaning happy. That will do, mother. I see Sylvia will be always a sore subject with you, and a bone of contention between us. But I must make the best of it. My affection for you shall not be diminished by your prejudice, nor my love for Sylvia lessened because you refuse to love her.'

He went upstairs to his room, the fresh bright English room, with its English comforts. There was a fire burning in his dressing-room to welcome the voyager from a warmer climate. But this material luxury could not restore Edmund Standen's good temper. He flung himself into the arm-chair before the fire, and sat there in gloomy meditation instead of hastening to make his toilet for dinner.

'Domestic dissension!' he muttered, 'how hard it is! Will my mother never reconcile herself to my choice? Will this sort of thing continue for the rest of our lives? It tempts me to think that my mother's influence was at the bottom of that wretched letter.'

He went downstairs a quarter of an hour later, refreshed as to his external appearance, but by no means comfortable in his mind. The three ladies were already assembled in the dining-room, and Mrs. Sargent was looking almost bright, now that she was once more under the mother's wing. But Mrs. Standen and Esther both had a cloudy look. Except for their first greeting Edmund and Esther had hardly spoken to each other once since his return. Miss Rochdale looked very small, and slight, and insignificant in her black dress, and seemed anxious to avoid Edmund's notice.

The dinner progressed in the usual stately manner —that respectable stateliness and slowness which makes even a moderate dinner such a lengthy business. It would have been pleasant enough if there had been plenty of talk to fill the pauses in the service, but this was rather a silent party. Ellen and her mother talked a little, in confidential tones, chiefly about the lamented deceased, and the details of his sudden end. Edmund, whom inclination would have kept silent, felt that for civility's sake he must talk to Esther.

'Anything stirring at Hedingham while I was away?' he asked. 'Have you any news to tell me, Esther? You ought to have quite a budget after three months.'

Miss Rochdale blushed, and looked down at her plate.

'I don't think there's much to tell,' she said. 'Hedingham is always quiet, you know, Edmund.'

'Yes, it's a dreadfully dead and alive place, no doubt; still in three months there must have been some remarkable events—cricket matches, football——'

'I really don't know anything about cricket or football.'

'Dinner parties, births, deaths, marriages?'

At this last word Esther's blush deepened to such crimson that Edmund could but remark it.

'Come, there has been a wedding,' he exclaimed, 'and one that you are rather interested in, I should think, by the way you blush. What does it mean,

Esther? Have you been getting married yourself, and kept the news to surprise me on my
return?'

'No, Edmund. I am never going to marry. I've
been making a solemn vow to that effect to the
little ones upstairs. I'm going to be Aunt Esther
all my life, and a nice old maiden aunt by-and-by.'

'Nice you must always be; but we shan't allow
you to be always a spinster. My mother must have
some of the propensities of her sex, superior-minded
as she is. Now, you know, all women are match-
makers. When they've done with matrimonial
schemes on their own account they begin to plot
for some one else. I've no doubt my mother has
her views about you.'

Esther was silent, and looked even a little embar-
rassed by this mild badinage.

' Then there is positively no news in Hedingham?'
said Edmund.

' None that you would care to hear.'

Dinner was over at last, and the produce of the
Dean House grapery duly praised—the largest
bunches sent upstairs to the children by the fond
grandmother. Edmund left the room with his
mother, put his arm through hers, and led her towards the study, a snug little room where there were

always candles ready to be lighted when any one wanted to write a letter or find a book.

'Come in here, mother,' said the young man. 'I want to have a long talk. I suppose it's too late for me to go to the schoolhouse to-night, though I had set my heart upon seeing Sylvia before I went to bed. Our dinner is always such a long business.'

He struck a match, lighted the tall candles in the old silver candlesticks, wheeled a comfortable chair forward for his mother, and then seated himself opposite her.

'Now, mother,' he said, 'I've dined and rested, in obedience to your behest, and now tell me all about Sylvia.'

'Edmund,' faltered Mrs. Standen, looking at him with unspeakable tenderness, 'I have something to tell you which will, I fear, make you very unhappy, yet it ought not to do so, if you can only be wise, and see the matter as I see it. You have had a most happy escape.'

'What do you mean?' cried Edmund, with quickened breathing. 'I don't understand a word you say.'

'Sylvia Carew is married.'

'Married?' he cried, looking at her in sheer amazement, and then he broke out into a laugh, singularly harsh of sound as compared with that genial laughter which was natural to him. 'Come, mother, this is a joke, of course. Or you're trying me—you want to find out how I should take the loss of her, were it possible for me to lose her. But it isn't possible, except by death.' Then, with an awful look he cried out, 'She's not dead, is she? You said just now that she was well, but you may have been paltering with me in a double sense. The dead are well. For God's sake, speak,' he cried violently, 'is Sylvia dead?'

'No, she is well enough, as I told you when you asked about her; and she is what the world calls wonderfully fortunate. She is married to Sir Aubrey Perriam.'

'Mother, do you want to drive me mad? Whose invention, whose lie is this? Married to Sir Aubrey! Why, she had never seen the man's face. I heard her say so the day before the school feast.'

'True, but he saw her at the school feast; saw her and fell in love with her. They were married about five weeks after you left. A very quiet marriage. No one, except the Vicar and the people concerned, knew anything about it till it was over. It was a nine days' wonder. They came back to the Place a fortnight ago. I have seen Lady Perriam driving about in her carriage.'

'Lady Perriam,' cried Edmund, with a still harsher laugh. 'How well it sounds, doesn't it? I suppose it was for that she married a man who must be nearly old enough to be her grandfather. Lady Perriam! No, it was her father forced her to marry him. I'll not believe that she was base. I know that she loved me. I heard the beating of her heart in the moment of our parting—the heart that beat so strongly, and seemed all truth. I know that she loved me!'

'She may have loved you in her own selfish way; but you see she loved rank and wealth much better.'

'It was no act of her own free will. She was goaded to it, forced to do it.'

'She renounced you of her own free will in less than a week after you left,' answered Mrs. Standen; and then she told the story of her first and only visit to Sylvia Carew.

'Esther was present all the time; Esther heard all,' she said in conclusion.

'Oh, I am not going to question the truth of your statements,' returned Edmund wearily. 'She has married that old man—that is enough. It matters very little by what degrees she arrived at that baseness. Enough to know that she lied to me ; that when she **looked up in my** face with tearful **eyes**—those lovely eyes—and swore to be true to the very last, she was capable of deceiving me ; a fine house, a carriage, **a** high-sounding name, could tempt her away from **me. Say even** that her father persuaded her, threatened, tormented her, **had she been loyal she** would **have borne the** uttermost **torment, she** would have died under **the** torture, rather **than broken** her faith with **me.** The struggle would not have been for **very** long. She knew that **I** was **coming back. A** little courage, **a** little constancy, and I should have been at her side to claim **and hold her for** my own against all the world.'

The strong **man was** vanquished by **the force of** that stronger passion—and, for the **first** time since his father's death, Edmund Standen wept bitter tears.

The **mother flew to his** side, **knelt by** his chair, hung upon him fondly, trying to comfort him, with overflowing love.

' **Edmund,' she** sobbed, ' it is not my fault—you will not hate me because of this sorrow that has fallen upon you. Believe me, I did nothing to influence that false, wicked girl. I went to her, prepared **to take her** to my heart—I promised to be generous to you by-and-by, if she proved to be a good wife—I tried to conciliate her, but she was false to you in her heart at that very moment. She seized upon the shallowest pretext for jilting you. She is a base designing creature, not worth a thought.'

'Hush, mother,' said the young man, with an almost solemn quietude. He had dried those unmanly tears, and bore the sharp pains of this new sorrow like a martyr. 'Hush, mother—not one word against her. Let her name be dead between us. Let it be more utterly dead than the names of those we have loved and lost. We speak of them sometimes. We will never speak of her.'

His mother, wise even in her love, kissed his cold brow—damp with the anguish of this mental struggle—and left him alone with his sorrow. Whatever form his passion took, were it despair or anger, it was best that he should fight his battle alone.

CHAPTER VIII.

THE ALOE THAT BLOOMS BUT ONCE.

THE Dean House family saw no more of Edmund Standen that night. He stayed in the study for about an hour, and then let himself quietly out of the hall door, and set off in the direction of Hedingham. Some curious impulse of mind and heart led him to the scene of his lost happiness—the shadowy old churchyard where he had lingered with his beloved in the summer evenings that were gone, the wide-stretching old yew which had so often been their trysting tree—the garden hedge by which he had waited sometimes after dark for the stolen hand-clasp, a few hasty words, a promise of meeting to-morrow.

The moon was up, and the country side glorious in that solemn beauty which only moonlight can give. The distant line of sea yonder, which the lonely pedestrian saw from the hill top, looked silver white against the dark of wood and moor. Edmund crossed that little copse adjoining the hillside meadow, and the old chestnut tree, beneath which he and Sylvia had met so often.

The past is eternal, says Schiller. Edmund felt that his past happiness must colour all his life to come, never to be forgotten, an ever-present regret, a haunting shadow dividing him from all possibilities of joy. He lingered a little beneath the wide boughs of the chestnut. Early to blossom, early to fade, like his own hopes, had been the old tree. The dead leaves fluttered slowly down about him as he stood there, alone with his withered hopes. ' Poor leaves, poor dreams!' he said to himself; ' who would have thought in your spring tide that you bloomed but to decay?'

It was ten o'clock when Edmund entered the village, and Hedingham was for the most part asleep. The ripple of the brook that ran through the rustic street was the only sound in the place. There were lights in the vicarage windows, and lights in the school-house, lights gleaming from the two lattices he had watched so often. He crossed the churchyard, lingering a little by the tomb of the de Bossineys, as he had lingered under the chestnut. Here they two had parted, with vows of eternal fidelity. Here he had left her sorrow stricken.

'Fortune is a speedy consoler,' he said to himself bitterly.

He opened the loosely latched gate, between the churchyard and the schoolmaster's garden, and went in. He wanted to see James Carew—to task him with having forced his daughter to this ill-assorted union—to tell him in no gentle phrase his opinion of that act.

He knocked at the low door under the porch, and it was opened promptly. But not by James Carew. The person who opened it was a youngish man, with sandy hair, and spectacles.

'Is Mr. Carew at home?' asked Edmund, wondering who this stranger might be.

'Mr. Carew left Hedingham six weeks ago,' answered the young man. 'He gave up the situation of schoolmaster, partly on account of declining health and partly because of his daughter having married Sir Aubrey Perriam.'

'Do you know where Mr. Carew has gone?'

'Not exactly, sir. I believe he went abroad, somewhere in the south of France, to spend the winter.'

This seemed curious. Edmund fancied that Sylvia's father would remain at Hedingham to profit by the barter of his daughter's peace; yet

it had been foolishness to expect to find him still
a parish schoolmaster toiling for a pittance. That
would have been a sorry bargain which would have
left him no better off than before. He had doubtless hurried off to enjoy life, remote from the scene
of his iniquity.

Edmund left the schoolhouse. It had a changed.
look to him somehow, as if it were but the dead
corpse of the place he had once known. The garden
was strewed with faded leaves—the dahlias and
ragged chrysanthemums spoke of autumn and decay
—the perfume of the summer was fled—scentless
flowers bloomed coldly in the beds that had once
been sweet with roses and carnations, sweet peas, and
mignonette.

' How shall I teach myself to forget her ?' thought
Edmund, as he walked homeward to begin common
daily life again, without the charm that had
sweetened it.

He had been happy enough before he had met
Sylvia Carew, but now happiness seemed impossible
without her.

Mrs. Standen and Esther were both agreeably surprised by Edmund's manner next morning. They
had fancied that the gloom of this great sorrow
would hang over him long, would poison his life for

years to come. They had thought, with fear and trembling, how some perilous fever of mind and body might be the issue of his disappointment. They were unspeakably relieved to find him in outward bearing almost the same as of old; a little graver and more silent perhaps, but manly, cheerful, thoughtful for others. In a word, Edmund Standen did not wear his heart upon his sleeve for daws to peck at.

Yet in his innermost heart he felt that all the best and brightest part of his life was ended. The hopes and dreams that had made youth so fair a morning were dead for ever. He nerved himself to face this grief and conquer it, or at least rise superior to it; but the grief was none the less intense because he bore it like a man. He also felt it like a man, to the core of his wounded heart.

He had a long serious talk with his mother the day after his return. They walked up and down the broad gravel mall together in the cheerful autumn sunlight, and spoke of many things, but not a word of Sylvia.

'I think I shall go back to the Continent, mother, and wander about for a year or two,' said Edmund; 'there's a great deal of Northern Europe that I should like to see—Roumania, Hungary, Poland.

I might stop away as much as three years, perhaps.'

'Very well, Edmund,' said his mother, in her firm yet gentle voice. 'If it is really for your happiness that you should go, I cannot say stop. But I am getting old, and I had hoped you would have been my friend and companion in declining life. It seems hard that you must run away from me just when I need you most. Do you think it will be so much easier to get rid of your trouble in a foreign land— that you can dig a deeper grave for sorrow in a strange soil ?'

'You are right, mother. Trees and hills and flowers, and every wind and angle in the road, remind me of—what has been. But they do not awaken memory. That never sleeps, never can sleep. I daresay I should be just as wretched in Germany. If my going away would grieve you, why I'll stop.'

'If it would grieve me, Edmund! What have I to live for except you? Poor Ellen and the children —and Esther. They are very dear to me, but they have always been secondary to you. I gave you my whole heart, Edmund.'

'Yet you would have disinherited me.'

'That was a desperate means to save you from a

fatal step.   Providence has interfered.   I shall never talk of disinheriting you any more.'

'If you knew how little I value money, you would better understand how vain a threat that was.   Fate has been on your side, mother, but I could have held my own against all the world.   I care less for money now ; and yet I feel that I can't lead an idle life. The dawdling, half-asleep and half-awake existence of a country squire won't do for me.   I should go out of my mind.   If you will not let me go abroad and roam from one place to another, I must find some kind of employment.'

'My dear boy, I only desire to see you happy.'

'I believe that, mother,' the son answered tenderly, 'and to be happy I must be occupied; hard work is the best cure for my disease.   I'll go to Monkhampton to-morrow morning, see Sanderson, the manager, and get him to take me into the bank. I fancy I must have inherited some of my father's commercial capacity.'

'Dear Edmund, there is so little occasion for you to do anything.   You will have as good an income as you can possibly desire.'

'I want employment, mother, not income.   If I were a heaven-born genius I should go up to London and read for the bar, but I don't feel that I could

wait seven years for my first brief. I'd rather have
a stool in the Monkhampton bank, and count the
farmers' greasy notes. I should feel that I was
doing something.'

'Ah, Edmund, I look forward to the day when
you will see things in a new light. When a hope
that I once fondly cherished may perhaps be
realized.'

'What hope, mother?'

'The hope of seeing you united to an amiable and
worthy wife.'

'Stop, mother. Let that subject be a sealed book.
I shall never marry.'

'Never is a long word, Edmund.'

'But life is not long. You know what my
favourite poet says—"Our brief life forbids the
indulgence of a distant hope." What is to-day
with me will be to-morrow.'

'If I thought that I should me miserable. But
I trust in the goodness of God. My beloved son
will not always be unhappy. The leaves fall from
yonder trees, Edmund, but spring will bring new
buds.'

'The heart of man has not the same happy
facility for putting forth new shoots. Man's heart is
like the aloe, which blossoms once in a generation.'

'My dear Edmund, it is natural for you to feel as you do. Yes, you shall take a situation at the bank; you shall work as hard as you like; only stay near me. Life is indeed too brief for the severance of a mother from her only son. I will put my trust in Providence, and wait till the aloe blossoms again.'

'Not this aloe, mother. It may grow into a good strong plant, and be of some use in its generation, but it shall put forth no second flower.'

'Who shall answer for the heart? Only God and time,' answered the mother solemnly.

This conversation was not without a consoling effect upon Edmund. He went to the Monkhampton bank next day, and as it was only his caprice to seek employment, and salary was not a matter of bread and cheese to him, he was received by the manager with open arms. Mr. Sanderson was glad to pay honour to the representative of the founders of the bank. He offered Edmund a place immediately, and a hundred and fifty pounds per annum to start with. 'It seems absurd to talk to you of salary,' said Mr. Sanderson grandly, 'but a hundred and fifty pounds will give you an extra hunter in the course of the year, or pay for your gloves.'

'You're very kind,' answered Edmund, 'but I

don't want hunters or gloves. I want employment and independence.'

'Rather a curious business,' thought the manager, when the applicant had retired. 'I suppose he has had another shindy with the old lady. They said that mother and son quarrelled about the schoolmaster's pretty daughter, whom Sir Aubrey Perriam was foolish enough to marry. But what is the present row about, I wonder ?'

The manager was surprised when Mrs. Standen drove up to the door in her pony-carriage to fetch her son after his first day at the bank. Still more surprised to see the mother's look of love as Edmund joined her.

'Come to fetch her little boy home from day school,' said Mr. Sanderson to himself, 'then there has been no shindy after all, and the young man means business.'

CHAPTER IX.

LADY PERRIAM had been married three months.
Two out of those three months she had spent at
Perriam Place, and it seemed to her that her
existence as Sir Aubrey's wife was quite an old
thing. 'Lady Perriam. Sylvia, Lady Perriam,'
she repeated the title to herself wonderingly sometimes. There was so small a difference between
Lady Perriam and Sylvia Carew. The same dis-
content, the same unsatisfied yearnings gnawed
Sylvia's heart, amidst the placid grandeurs of
Perriam Place as in the village schoolhouse. Her
ambition had been gratified beyond her wildest
dream, but its gratification had brought her so
little.

For a short time, just so long as novelty, like
the bloom upon a peach, gave charm and beauty
to her surroundings, she had believed it all-sufficient

for content, nay for happiness, to be mistress of
Perriam Place; to be able to say, 'my house, my
dressing-room, my boudoir, my gardens, my servants;' to be waited upon by respectful attendants;
to have a carriage at her command; and to be called
'My lady.' It was also very pleasant to have no
rooms to clean, no dinners to cook, no cups and
saucers or plates and dishes to wash after every
meal—in a word, no daily routine of domestic
labour. These were all on the debit side of her
ledger. But on the other side the sum of her dis-
contents swelled day by day. Novelty's brief bloom
soon faded from Perriam Place; the large empty
rooms began to wear a dreary look; nay, at times,
when she had been long alone in the drawing-room,
there grew upon her a sense of some ghostly unseen
presence lurking in the background of that spacious
saloon. She almost feared to look behind her chair
lest she should see something; what, she had never
imagined to herself. Sometimes she would glance
nervously at one of those seven long windows, half
fearing to see a strange face looking in at her—a
face not of this earth. Perhaps the vicinity of so
many dead Perriams in the little churchyard below
the Italian garden may have had something to do
with this fancy.

This stately solitude seen from the outside would have seemed perfect **to** the girlish eyes of Sylvia Carew. It was the life that she would have asked for had some liberal fairy bade her choose her **own** destiny. But how many of us would choose amiss were we permitted to select our **own** lot out of the **urn of fate. He who** shakes the lots in **the urn** alone knows what is good for us.

That splendid life, set round with worldly pomp, **was** very dismal for Sir Aubrey Perriam's young **wife.** Sweet though it was to be free from menial labour, the days seemed long and empty without that sordid toil. Sylvia **laid out a** grand scheme for completing her education. She would **read the** Latin poets, with the aid of grammar **and** lexicon ; she would improve her German. Unhappily, schemes **such as these are apt to** break down where there is no one to supervise the studies, or sympathize with **the** student. Sylvia had worked desperately at German during Edmund Standen's brief courtship, so that she might read the books he admired, and talk **to him a little** in that rugged language which has a force and power hardly found in more melodious tongues. Edmund **had** read Schiller's ballads to her sometimes in their twilight dawdlings by streamlet or meadow ; and to please

him by her progress she had worked assiduously,
and deemed the labour sweet. Now she yawned
over the strong wine of that verse, as if it had
been the weakest milk and water of the Words-
worthian school — infinitely diluted Wordsworth.
Nor did Horace's odes, which had seemed full of
grace and meaning when Edmund declaimed and
explained them, now appear anything more than a
string of nouns and adjectives, ablative absolutes
and gerundives, worked into a distracting tangle.

She might have obtained some kind of assistance
from Mordred, but, whenever she ventured to appeal
to that authority, he meandered off into prosy
criticism upon the bard, and insisted on entertaining Sylvia with a catalogue of editions. His own
understanding was too weak for a teacher. He
could only repeat what he had read. Thus, after
a month or so of systematic study, Lady Perriam
lost heart, and only took up her books in a desultory manner.

Sir Aubrey gave her no encouragement to study.
He had the old-fashioned notion that a young
woman should know how to make what his grandfather had called 'puddens,' and be great in the
still-room. If she hankered after higher accom-
plishments, she should paint flowers and butter-

flies upon velvet, or draw minute landscapes in pencil, to the injury of her sight, or paint feathers in the same minute style to adorn her friends' albums. Then to fill up the sum of her industrious days she might do tambour work, or Abraham and Isaac in tent-stitch, as the last Lady Perriam but one had done, a work of art which might be seen to this day in the Bolingbroke chamber. Of blue stockings Sir Aubrey had a pious horror.

'Look at Lady Mary Wortley Montagu,' he said, when he dissuaded Sylvia from the study of the Latin poets; 'she was vastly clever, but hardly respectable even at her best; and if the scandals of the period are to be believed, not over-clean.'

For music, vocal or instrumental, Sir Aubrey cared not a jot. He had bought a cottage piano at Sylvia's request, and it was permitted to stand in a corner by one of the fireplaces in the saloon, where, in his heart of hearts, the baronet deemed it an eyesore. He would ask Sylvia to sing to him every evening, in exactly the same courteous tone ; but he read the paper while she sang, and was rarely aware of the subject of her minstrelsy. Yet he thanked her with undeviating politeness when she closed the piano.

The monotony of life at Perriam Place was far

beyond anything one could expect in a monastery. Those solemn abodes are subject to the intrusion of travellers, the inspection of a vicar-general, changes in administration even, feast days, fast days, retreats, an endless variety as compared with life at Perriam, which was smooth and changeless as the bosom of a canal. The well-trained servants prepared and set forth each day's meals in the same order. The same stillness pervaded the stately mansion from day to day. The endless ticking of the Louis Quartorze clock in the hall—a clock whose lacquered case was emblazoned with all the quarterings of the Perriams—seemed like a re-minder of eternity. 'Always the same, always the same,' said that solemn time-piece in Sylvia's weary ear. *Semper eadem, semper eadem.*

Sir Aubrey was never unkind to her; but, on the other hand, he was not the indulgent husband she had expected him to be. He was in no manner her slave; but, on the contrary, expected and exacted perpetual obedience from her. He was rather like a kind father than a doting husband. He did not lavish his wealth upon her caprices, and indeed rarely granted her requests—though he always refused them with amiability.

One day she ventured to suggest that they might

lead a gayer life than their present existence, that Perriam Place would seem all the pleasanter if it were occasionally filled with visitors. Sir Aubrey raised his eyebrows in placid astonishment.

'My love, are you not happy?' he asked.

Sylvia sighed, and replied that she was perfectly happy.

'Then why hazard our happiness by introducing a foreign element into our lives? You have not been accustomed to a house full of visitors, neither have I. Since we are both happy, let us do our best to remain so.'

Thus spoke the voice of age and wisdom, but youth's rebellious heart revolted against this sage decree. Tears of vexation started to Sylvia's eyes.

'I knew you lived here like a hermit while you were a bachelor,' she said; 'people used to talk enough about it. But I thought when you were married it would be different—that you would entertain the county people as other rich men do, and enjoy life a little.'

'I hope the prospect of entertaining the county people was not your sole inducement to become my wife,' answered Sir Aubrey, with that air of offended dignity with which he armed himself at times as with a hauberk. 'As to enjoying life, I live my own life, which is to my mind the highest enjoyment possible to humanity.'

Sylvia shrugged her shoulders, and submitted. She was obliged to submit, had indeed discovered that life matrimonial was all submission. Sir Aubrey was a kind, but not an indulgent, husband. That enthusiasm which had led him to woo and wed a village schoolmaster's daughter had cooled a little now that she was his wife—his own property to the end of his days. It was not that he was in any manner disappointed, or that his admiring affection for Sylvia had grown cold. He was perfectly satisfied with his lot, supremely pleased with his fair young wife; but he meant to live his own life, and meant also that she should conform to that life, and not seek strange pleasures and amusements which would inflict trouble and vexation, as well as expense, upon him.

The Perriam honeymoon had been a very quiet business. The *entresol* in the Faubourg St. Honoré was not the palatial home which Sylvia had supposed so great a man as Sir Aubrey would inhabit even in the land of the stranger. Sir Aubrey had taken his bride to all the usual shows—the Louvre, Luxembourg, the grand old churches, the *Jardin des*

Plantes, the Hotel Cluny, Napoleon's Mausoleum, the fountains at Versailles, and the long terrace at St. Germains. All these things Sir Aubrey had shown her; but, wonderful and beautiful as they seemed to the untravelled rustic, a shadow of dulness hung over them all. The numerous churches tired her before she had seen half of them. The vast palaces with their endless pictures palled upon her weary senses. Sir Aubrey, with every wish to be kind, instructive, and explanatory, always contrived to bring her away from the objects which most interested her. He marched her from place to place. There was no lounging, no pleasant loitering. No long, sultry day dawdled away in that deep wood at St. Germains. Yet Sylvia fancied that she and Edmund might have so wasted a day had they two been bride and bridegroom.

Sir Aubrey took his wife to the *Théâtre Français* on one solitary occasion to see Molière's *Femmes Savantes*, but vetoed all other theatres as disreputable.

The weather was sultry during the greater part of Sylvia's honeymoon, and the wide streets of the wonderful city were dim with a warm vapour that whispered of fever and cholera. Sir Aubrey's habits were early, and the evening, the only period when Paris is tolerable in summer time, was a period of

imprisonment for Sylvia. She was playing chess
with her husband in the stifling little saloon by the
light of a pair of wax candles, while the city was gay
with many voices, and music, and light, yonder on
the boulevards where the night wind blew freshly,
and when people who knew how to make the best of
life were eating ices at the rustic café in the cascade
in the bois. Sylvia went back to England with the
impression that Paris was a splendid city, but not
a gay one.

They returned to Perriam Place, and Sylvia received the homage and obeisance of the household;
and in the moment of that triumph it seemed to her
an all-sufficing joy to be mistress of Perriam and
all these dependants. Whatever surprise these
domestics had felt at their lord's strange marriage
had been carefully smoothed out of their faces. They
welcomed James Carew's daughter as respectfully as
they could have welcomed Lady Guinivere herself.

Those improvements and alterations which Sylvia
had planned with so much satisfaction before her
marriage were not yet put in hand. Indeed a very
short space of married life had shown Lady Perriam
how little power she had over her lord, and how
little liberty of action she was likely to enjoy; and,
perhaps even worse than this, how small was to be

her command of money. She knew that her husband had wealth that exceeded his expenditure by tenfold, yet she derived neither pleasure nor power from his riches.

He looked unutterable surprise the first time she asked him for money.

'My dear child, what can you want with money?' he asked, as if they had been on a desert island where the circulating medium was useless.

'I—I should like a little to spend,' Sylvia answered, childishly. She had not forgotten that wretched woman in Bell-alley, Fetter-lane. Tenderness of heart was not Sylvia's strong point, yet it irked her to live amidst all these solid splendours, satiated with temporal comforts, and to feel that in all likelihood her mother was starving.

'To spend for the mere pleasure of spending,' said Sir Aubrey, like a wise father—one of dear Maria Edgeworth's model parents, for instance—remonstrating with his little girl. 'My dear Sylvia, is not that rather a childish reason?'

'But I didn't mean to say that. Of course, I want the money, or I shouldn't have asked you for it. I thought you would give me an allowance, perhaps, when we were married.'

'I have thought of that,' replied Sir Aubrey, as if

it were a matter demanding profound consideration,
' and I intend to do so—ultimately. But really your
wants must be infinitesimal. You have the dresses
and other garments you bought before our marriage.'

'The dresses are getting shabby,' said Sylvia. 'I
wore them all the time we were in Paris.'

'A month,' said Sir Aubrey. 'I have worn this
coat nearly eighteen months.'

'Then it's time you had a new one,' cried Sylvia,
sorely tried. 'But I'll go on wearing my shabby
dresses, if you like. It doesn't much matter; I
never see any one except you and Mordred.'

'I hope you have sufficient respect for me to dress
as nicely to please me as you would to win the
admiration of strangers,' returned Sir Aubrey, with
his offended air.

'I can't dress nicely without money to buy
clothes,' replied Sylvia. 'Women's dresses are not
like men's coats—they don't wear everlastingly.'

'Then it's a pity women do not adopt more substantial materials. Neither the linsey-woolseys our
grandmothers wore for use, nor the brocades which
they kept for state occasions, required to be renewed
every three months. The chairs in our bedroom
are covered with dresses of my grandmothers.
However, it is not your fault that the age is

frivolous, and I can't be angry with you for following the fashion of your day. 'I'll give you a cheque for twenty pounds, and before that is gone I will arrange your allowance of pocket money. There, my love, don't let me see any more tears in those pretty eyes.'

Sir Aubrey wrote the cheque, and fancied that he had acted with supreme liberality.

Sylvia sent half this money to Mrs. Carford, in the shape of a ten-pound note. She bought a dark silk dress with the remaining ten pounds, for, having talked of wanting a new dress, she was obliged to show Sir Aubrey that she had bought one.

Shortly after this the baronet informed his wife graciously that he had decided upon allowing her two hundred a year, payable quarterly, for her personal expenditure, and this he evidently considered a most liberal allowance. Sylvia thanked him warmly, and was indeed grateful for anything which should be hers without question. All her dreams of refurnishing the library, and replacing the faded curtains in the saloon with amber satin, were quite over. She knew that in Sir Aubrey she had found a new master. It was a more exalted bondage than her servitude to her father, but it was bondage all the same.

CHAPTER X.

TIME wears the beauty off all temporal blessings. That stately old yellow chariot, which had been at first a source of pride to Lady Perriam, by degrees became almost loathsome, so dismal were her lonely drives. Sir Aubrey preferred pottering about his farms on Splinter to promenades in the yellow chariot, so Sylvia had that equipage to herself and her own thoughts. It was like a state prison upon wheels. Beautiful as was the scenery round Perriam Sylvia soon grew weary of nature's loveliness. Before she had been a month at the Place she knew the landscape by heart, the hill-sides from which she saw the distant sea, the ferny lanes down which the great coach went staggering and rumbling, into pastoral valleys, whose cob-walled cottages looked the chosen abodes of peace and contentment.

Lady Perriam looked at those rustic houses with a

strange perplexed feeling. She had not been happy when she lived in a cottage, yet now that she inhabited a mansion it seemed to her as if those humbler dwellings must hold the secret of happiness. She was very lonely. Her lord's society gave her no delight, the park and gardens of Perriam Place became as a desert to her weary eyes. She paced the Italian terrace day after day, and, looking down at the peaceful graveyard below the marble balustrade, envied those Perriams who no longer knew life's weariness.

The few county families with whom Sir Aubrey condescended to maintain a tepid acquaintance paid their formal visits to the new mistress of the Place, and were not a little surprised at the graceful ease of manner with which Lady Perriam received them. She was in no wise abashed by these magnates of the land. But others came as well as the county people. Mrs. Toynbee and her two over-dressed daughters were among the earliest of Sylvia's visitors. The manufacturer's wife came with the intention of patronizing Lady Perriam, but was not slow to discover from Sylvia's icy reception that patronage was not exactly the tone to take here.

' We always said you would marry well, my dear,'

said Mrs. Toynbee, almost taking credit to herself for Sylvia's elevation. 'You had an air so far above your station.'

'My father was a gentleman before he was a parish schoolmaster,' answered Lady Perriam coolly. 'I never pretended to a higher station than that of a gentleman's daughter.'

'Of course not, my love; but you know there are lines of demarcation. Every one could see how superior you and Mr. Carew were, yet the gentry couldn't associate with you quite on equal terms, however much they might wish it. I'm sure I, for one, would have been charmed to have you at my parties—quite an ornament to them—but one's friends make such remarks if one steps ever so little way over the boundary line.'

'Yes, Mrs. Toynbee, no doubt persons of your position must be punctilious. The trading classes are full of narrow-minded prejudices; but with people of Sir Aubrey's rank it is quite different. Their position is not dependent on any one's approval or opinion. My carriage has been waiting for the last half-hour, Mrs. Toynbee,' added Lady Perriam, ringing the bell. 'Will you permit me to wish you good morning?' And the magnificent Mrs. Toynbee, the richest woman in Hedingham parish, found herself bowed out by the village schoolmaster's daughter.

'Did you ever see such insolence?' cried this outraged female as she spread out her silken flounces in the amplitude of their splendour, and settled herself in her luxurious landau, new from the coach-builder's, and with all the latest improvements in landaus.

'Of course not, ma, but you might have saved us such a humiliation if you'd taken my advice,' retorted Juliana Toynbee acrimoniously.

'Nasty thing!' exclaimed Edith, the second sister, meaning Lady Perriam.

'To treat us like that when I was going to be a friend to her, out of right down charity,' continued Mrs. Toynbee. 'What can she know about giving dinner-parties, or any of the things that become her station? What she wants is a clever and experienced friend at her elbow, to put her in the way of doing things in the right style. My dinners have been talked of from one end of the county to the other, and I shouldn't have minded any trouble to put her in the right way if she had shown herself commonly grateful.'

'It isn't in her to be grateful,' returned Juliana; 'and as to visiting at Perriam, I wouldn't darken her doors if she was to send us a formal invitation once a week. Besides, every one knows Sir Aubrey is as close as he well can be, and I don't suppose she'll ever have the chance of giving parties.'

And thus these ladies drove home, talking of Sylvia all the way, very warm as to their tempers, and very flushed as to their 'faces, and it was solemnly voted in the Toynbee household that Sylvia, Lady Perriam, was to be counted among the dead.

The day came when Sylvia was to see Edmund Standen for the first time since that sorrowful parting by the tomb of the de Bossineys. She heard of his return soon after it happened; heard of it from the lips of Mr. Bain, who announced the fact carelessly enough, yet contrived to watch the effect of that announcement upon Sylvia. One bright hectic spot flamed in the delicate cheek, but faded before Sir Aubrey had time to notice it.

' Mr. Standen has gone into the bank,' said the steward, not unwilling to prolong the discussion. ' The Western Union, as they call it, since it's been made a joint-stock bank. It has set people talking a little. Nobody thought young Standen would have gone into business. He has plenty to live upon, or will have after his mother's death, though

I believe at present he is quite dependent on the old lady.'

' I feel no interest in Mr. Standen or his affairs,' remarked the baronet, with dignity; so Mr. Bain said no more.

For several Sundays after their arrival at the Place Sylvia and her husband attended the little church in the dell, where a mild incumbent performed two services every Sunday, for the enlightenment of a sparse congregation drawn from adjacent hamlets. Then came a fine sunny Sabbath at the beginning of December, and Sir Aubrey proposed that they should go to church at Hedingham. ' I like Vancourt's sermons better than Smallman's,' said the baronet. ' We may as well drive over to Hedingham.'

Sylvia felt a kind of catch in her throat, which prevented her saying yes or no to this proposition. She should see him again then, that Edmund Standen whom she had once sworn to love eternally. She dreaded seeing him, yet desired to see him, to look on the unforgotten face, were it but for a moment.

The church looked bright and gay on that wintry morning, bright with the cheerful December sunshine. , Sir Aubrey owned a large square pew in

the chancel, which was the most aristocratic part of
the edifice; a pew placed as near the altar rails as it
could be placed, in a manner within the sanctuary;
a pew that was sumptuously provided with crimson
cushions, luxurious footstools, prayer books of
largest type, bound in faded crimson russia, and
emblazoned with the Perriam coat of arms—prayer
books in which good King George and a string of
princes and princesses, whose names are history,
were prayed for assiduously.

These chancel pews were on a slightly higher
level than the body of the church, and from Sir
Aubrey's pew Sylvia commanded a full view of the
Dean House party, who occupied a front pew in the
central aisle. There they all were: Mrs. Standen;
the delicate-looking widow from Demerara, with a
little girl of six years old at her side; Esther, and
Edmund; all in mourning, a very sombre-looking
party.

Not once during the service did Edmund's eyes
wander in Sylvia's direction, yet she felt that he was
aware of her presence. Those dark eyes of his
were for the most part bent rigidly upon his book.
Sylvia remembered his old manner, which, though
devout, was scarcely so attentive to the mere letter
of the service.

Sir Aubrey and his wife left the church by a little side door; it was one of the privileges of the chancel people to use this door; but in the churchyard Sir Aubrey was button-holed by a brother landowner, and while they were standing in the narrow path, close by that too well-remembered monument of the de Bossineys, Edmund and Esther Rochdale passed them. For one moment only the young man looked at Sylvia. Such a look! Contempt so scathing is not often expressed in one brief flash from disdainful eyes, one curve of a scornful lip. Deadly pale, yet with a look of unshaken firmness, her jilted lover passed her by, and the sharpest pain her heart had power to feel Sylvia felt at that moment.

' I hope I may never see him again,' she thought, as the yellow chariot bore her back to Perriam; ' never, unless I were free to win back his love. I know I could win it, though he may despise me now, if I were only free to try.' And she looked at Sir Aubrey, and began to speculate how long a man of that age might live—five years—ten—fifteen— twenty perhaps. Who could tell for what length of years an existence so placid and temperate as Sir Aubrey's might flow smoothly on ?

Did she wish him dead ? Did a thought so dark as to be in itself a crime ever enter her heart ? It had come but too near that with Lady Perriam. She had never shaped an actual wish, but she had calculated the measure of her husband's days, and had pictured to herself what might happen when he should take his rest with those other Perriams in the churchyard in that green hollow, where harts-tongue fern pushed its curved leaves between the crumbling stones of the old gray wall.

What a marvellous change that one event of Sir Aubrey's death would make in her existence! She would have five thousand a year, her very own, to squander as she pleased, instead of a pittance of two hundred a year doled out to her quarterly. And she would be free—free to recover Edmund Standen's love, were it possible for him to forgive her.

' I don't believe he could be angry with me very long,' she thought, ' or that he could shut his heart against me. He would remember those happy summer evenings. All the past would come back to him in a breath, and all his love with it.'

There was one fear which tortured Sylvia whenever her thoughts drifted that way. What if Edmund should marry Esther Rochdale? She felt sure that Esther was fond of him. She had made up her mind about that long ago; and it was an understood thing in Hedingham, where people knew, or affected to know, the most secret desires of their neighbours, that Mrs. Standen wished to see those two married. What more likely than that she would now try to patch up an engagement between them?

'His sister will help her no doubt,' thought Sylvia, ' and between them they will worry him into marrying that little dark thing.'

She remembered Esther's winning gentleness, her soft dark eyes with their pensive pleading look; not a girl against whom a man could steel his heart for ever, one might think.

The idea of this possibility added a new sting to Lady Perriam's keen regret. It made even the dulness of her life more bitter. She was glad to keep Mary Peter in her dressing-room for an hour's chat now and then, when that young person brought her home some new garment, and to hear her gossip about the Hedingham people, and sometimes a little about the occupants of Dean House.

Sir Aubrey happened to interrupt this friendly gossip one day, and after Mary Peter had retired, frozen by the baronet's urbanity, he expressed himself somewhat strongly upon the subject of his wife's familiarity with a village mantua-maker.

'I was not familiar with her,' pleaded Sylvia. 'I let her talk—that was all.'

'My love, to let a person of that kind tattle is to be familiar with her. It presupposes an interest in her conversation which it ought to be impossible for you to feel.'

'She talks about people I used to see before I was married,' said Sylvia.

'But with whom you have nothing more to do, and in whom your interest ought to have ceased with your marriage. Pray never let me see that young woman again.'

'She makes my dresses,' remonstrated Sylvia; 'I don't see how I can get on without her.'

'Are you so childish as to suppose that there is only one dressmaker at your service? You can have your gowns made by Mrs. Bowker, of Monkhampton, a very proper person.'

Sylvia sighed and submitted. So Mary Peter, who could talk of Edmund, recalling memories that were at once sweet and sad, was banished from Perriam Place. Little as Sylvia had cared for this humble friend, she felt life more lonely without her occasional society. Her father was away still, rejoicing in the sunshine of a warmer sky, on the shores of the Mediterranean, just contriving to exist

at a third-rate boarding house, on his scanty income. He liked the shores of **the Mediterranean even under** the disadvantage of a limited **income,** much better than the village of Hedingham, **and had no inten-** tion of returning **to English rusticity yet awhile.** He wrote to **his** daughter **occasionally, not forgetting** to hint that any addition to his pittance which she **might be** inclined to make would be welcome.

Sir Aubrey had given one state dinner to those county people who had called upon his wife—a **dinner** distinguished by **a solemn** splendour, **but** almost as gloomy as that sepulchral banquet which the **Roman** tyrant Domitian **gave to his friends, where the** walls were hung with black, and the para- phernalia of death so closely represented, that many **of the amiable Cæsar's guests swooned away and** died in **real earnest, slain by the mere** horror of this ghastly jest.

After this state dinner there **were** no more gaieties **at** Perriam, but **Sir Aubrey took** his lovely young wife to three or four **feasts of the same** kind which his friends **gave in her honour.** This constituted **Sylvia's brief** experience of **the** polite world; for now came an event which was **to** exclude Sir Aubrey Perriam from society for **ever.**

CHAPTER XI.

' SO FAIR A FORM LODGED NOT A MIND SO ILL.'

SYLVIA had been married six months. February, the weariest month in a cheerless winter, was dragging slowly to its dismal end. A north-east wind shook the casements of Perriam Place. The leafless elms in the avenue tossed their ragged branches as in the writhings of despair, as if they ejaculated hopelessly, 'When is warmer weather coming?' 'When are we going to bud?' Even the monkey trees swayed and creaked before the blast. Only the cedars stood up, grimly stern, and defied the north-easter.

Very dreary had been that long winter to Lady Perriam. After the half-dozen dinner parties given in her honour at the Manor Houses, Granges, and Towers within fifteen miles of Perriam Place there had been no further gaiety of any kind. Even her solitary airings in the yellow chariot had been curtailed by the inclemency of the weather. There had been nothing for her to do but walk about the spacious old house, with its vast, empty, useless rooms, and speculate what it might have been under a different master.

'If fortune had given Edmund and me such a house, with Sir Aubrey's wealth, how delightful we would have made it! We could have filled these dismal corridors with pleasant people, and made that vault-like dining-room brilliant with light and fire, and bright eyes, and jewels, and splendid dresses. Every day would have brought some new pleasure.'

This was the drift of Sylvia's fancies very often as she paced the long music-room—which knew not the sound of music—on wet afternoons, when there was not one gleam of brightness in the leaden sky, hardly a glimmer of hope in her own life.

She had thought to taste all the pleasures of the world as Sir Aubrey's wife. With the baronet newly subjugated, and at her feet, it had seemed such an easy thing to rule him. She had hoped for a slave, and she had found a master; a stricter master then her father; for beneath Mr. Carew's sway she had been able to do pretty much as she pleased, so long as she administered to all his wants and gave him a well-cooked dinner. With Sir

Aubrey for her master she had her own way in hardly anything.

He was not unkind to her; and that made her bondage seem all the worse. She had no ground for complaint. Against that smooth tyranny rebellion was almost impossible. He forbade this, he advised that, but he was always suavity itself. He narrowed her life into so small a circle that a squirrel in a cage might have known as much of liberty. Friends or acquaintance she had none; for the county people who had been willing to take her by the hand had all fallen away, receiving no encouragement to be civil.

That severe winter tried Sir Aubrey's somewhat feeble constitution. He had a good deal of illness, and the stately gentleman who had seemed such a model of old-fashioned gallantry that warm summer afternoon in Mr. Hopling's orchard, was restless, fretful, and peevish when afflicted with influenza, or a mild attack of bronchitis. At these times Sir Aubrey preferred the ministrations of Jean Chapelain to those of his young wife, yet expected that Sylvia should spend a good deal of her time in the sick room, and liked her to read the political articles and foreign correspondence in *The Times* for his edification. She performed all her duties with a tolerable grace; but weariness was in her **heart** neverthe-less.

But if Sir Aubrey's society was at times a **burden** almost too heavy for impatient **youth to bear,** Mordred Perriam's **dulness** was still harder to **be** endured. **He was a more** fatiguing companion than his brother, inasmuch **as he talked a great** deal more. **He** was fond of **talking;** and the chief deprivation of **his** life hitherto had been the lack **of** listeners. He found Sylvia courteously attentive to his discourse. She did not wish to be rude to her husband's brother. So **he** at once seized upon her **as the** long-desired listener. He had just sense **enough to perceive her** intelligence; **and** he told himself that his dry-as-dust discourse would expand and improve her mind.

'You are not **like** ordinary young women, my dear,' he said, when Sylvia confessed her desire to learn Latin, and **to** know something of the classic writers. 'You can take an **interest in great subjects.'**

Day after day, evening after evening, he twaddled **on in the same** dull, dry way, shedding **no** ray of light from his own intellect upon the pages he pored **over, and whose contents it was his delight to** recapitulate. **He** was always finding little bits in **his** daily studies which he thought would interest Sylvia, and the little bits were usually the dullest passages in the prosings of some third-rate philosopher—the tritest axioms of morality, inflated into importance by grandiloquent language.

When the baronet was confined to his room, which happened often during that doleful winter, Mordred and Sylvia took their meals *tête-à-tête*, in the gloomy dining-room. The mild old bookworm would even desert his beloved kitchen garden to take his constitutional in Sylvia's company, shambling up and down the terrace, never ceasing from that even flow of prosiness. There were moments when Lady Perriam was wicked enough to wish him a sharer in that tranquil silence which ruled among the rest of his race in that hallowed ground in the dell.

Mordred's health was very little better than his brother's, but being a person of secondary importance the household took less notice of his ailments. He grumbled a little about himself from time to time; complained of pains here and twitches there; now pointed to his chest, and now to his head; but received little more attention from any one than if he had been some piece of household machinery slightly out of order.

'I know I shall die suddenly when my time

comes,' he said one day to Lady Perriam. 'It may be many years hence——'

'I dare say it will,' returned Sylvia, with an involuntary sigh.

'Or it may be much sooner than any one expects; but I feel a conviction that I shall go off without a moment's warning. There are a great many cases on record of men who had a prevision as to the manner of their death. I have my prevision. So many twitches and spasms as I suffer must have some significance. It may be that my heart is wrong; or the seat of disease may be in the brain. When you consider the delicate functions which the spinal marrow has to perform in relation to the cerebral matter, you can hardly wonder that the brain is apt to get out of order. When you look at the heart as a complicated pumping apparatus which is never permitted to rest, and not subject to repair, you cannot wonder that the machinery is liable to collapse. I have received warning from both directions, and I am prepared for the worst.'

'Mere fancy, I daresay, Mr. Perriam,' said Sylvia, with the serenity that springs from indifference.

'No, my dear, it is not fancy. But I am prepared for the worst. I have made my will.'

'Indeed,' murmured Sylvia, with a shade more

interest.   She thought it just possible that Mordred
intended to reward her endurance of his dulness by
the bequest of his worldly substance.

'Yes.   I bequeath my library—nearly five thousand volumes of solid and instructive literature—to
the Mechanics' Institute in Monkhampton.   I also
bequeath my estate, now yielding two hundred per
annum, but likely to improve with the lapse of
years, to trustees, for the benefit of the same insti-
tution.   They will build a wing for the reception of
the books; they will from time to time, as funds
accrue, collect other books always of a like character.
They will furthermore employ a librarian for the
care of the aforesaid books and any further collection,
as heretofore mentioned, at a salary of fifty pounds
per annum.'

Mordred was quoting verbatim from the will, a
document which he kept in his own possession, and
perused frequently with enjoyment.

'I have sometimes thought,' he added, graciously,
'that such a situation would suit a man of studious
habits, like your father.'

Christmas had been in no wise different from other
seasons at Perriam.   There was some customary
dole given to the poor, but this was done unobtru-
sively through the hands of the housekeeper, so that

the blessings of the recipients assailed not Sir Aubrey's ears. Christmas Day seemed an extra Sunday in the week, and that was all.

It was now two months after Christmas, and Sir Aubrey had been more or less ailing all the time. The Monkhampton surgeon who attended him declared there was no cause for alarm. The severe weather had been trying; Sir Aubrey was a little out of sorts, and so on; but with the coming of spring he would doubtless be himself again. Lady Perriam must not feel uneasy.

This Mr. Stimpson, the surgeon, an elderly man who enjoyed high repute in Monkhampton, said to Lady Perriam herself, in a cheery confidential tone.

'There is no danger then?' asked Lady Perriam thoughtfully.

'None whatever; a temporary derangement of the system, nothing more.'

'I am glad to hear that. I have sometimes thought that Sir Aubrey must be seriously ill. His memory seems to fail him a little now and then. He repeats things two or three times, and does not seem to know that he has said them before.'

Mr. Stimpson looked a little grave at this, but speedily recovered himself. It is a doctor's duty to be cheerful.   He brings to bear an amiable gaiety, by way of contrast to the gloom of sick-beds and incurable diseases.

Sylvia sat alone, absorbed in deepest thought for some time after the doctor had left her.   Sometimes, out of this illness of Sir Aubrey's, piercing the doleful shadows of the sick-room, there had arisen, pale with distance, the star of an unholy hope.   What if the end were nearer than she had ever deemed possible ?   What if her husband were doomed to die ere very long and leave her free to marry Edmund Standen ?

In her young life death had been, as yet, a stranger. She could not think of that dreadful presence as calmly as some to whom the fatal visitant has grown a familiar guest.   She thought with a shudder of the dark gulf, the mysterious, impenetrable grave, which lay between her and liberty.   Sir Aubrey had been a tyrant, but at the worst an unconscious despot.   He had never been intentionally unkind.   He had tried to shape the young, bright life to fit his own placid existence, had stifled all the natural aspirations of joy-loving youth, had made Sylvia's days a burden to her ; yet, after his own fashion, he had been kind.   It seemed almost impossible that she should wish for his death.

'I do not wish him dead,' she said to herself, when that possible release presented itself like a hope, 'but, if he dies, I shall win my love back again—my first and only love. I will make him forgive me, though I have sinned against him so deeply. I will make him trust me again, although I have been so false. I know that I have power to win him back.'

CHAPTER XII.

In the early part of March Sir Aubrey left his room.
He was now pronounced well enough to spend a few
hours in the saloon daily, and even to take a short
drive in the yellow chariot on a sunny day, when the
wind was in a genial quarter.

He was very glad to avail himself of these privileges, and made haste to abandon his invalid habits,
dressed himself as carefully as ever, and reappeared
with that gracious and patrician aspect which made
him look like one of Vandyke's portraits in modern
costume.

He thanked Sylvia courteously for her attention to
him during his illness, and was kinder than usual to
her, forbearing to criticise her conduct in trifles, and
to lecture.

'My dear,' he said, 'I have given you no present
since I put my mother's diamond keeper upon your
finger.   It belonged to her mother's mother, you

know, and has a higher value from association than from the worth of the stones, which are of the purest water, but small.'

Sylvia gave a little regretful sigh. She had once supposed that diamond hoop to be the forerunner of a shower of gifts, plenteous as that golden rain which descended on Danae.

'I have not given you jewels, Sylvia, partly because I do not care to see a woman bedizened with precious stones, but more because I do not wish to be associated in your mind with rich gifts. When I am dead and gone you will be rich—rich enough to be a prize for some adventurer, should you be so foolish as to marry again.'

Hereupon Sir Aubrey opened an oval morocco case, in which reposed on black velvet a necklace of single diamonds, each as large as a prize pea. The silver setting was so light as to be hardly visible. The necklace seemed a circlet of liquid light.

Sylvia's eye sparkled. She gave a gasp of mingled surprise and delight.

'How lovely !' she exclaimed.

'It is yours, my love,' answered the baronet, in his placid way. 'I bought the necklace for a duke's daughter ; but death stole my promised bride. I give it now to my true and kind wife.'

Lady Perriam, not easily melted, burst into tears.

‘ God keep me true to you, in thought and in deed,’ she cried passionately. ‘ But I am not worthy of your kindness.’

‘ You have been my patient nurse, my faithful companion,’ answered Sir Aubrey, gently. ‘ Dry your tears, my dear. A diamond necklace is not a thing to cry about.’

‘ I am very proud of your gift, it is more splendid than anything I ever dreamed of. But it is your kindness that touches me,’ said Sylvia.

She had remembered how mean she had thought him because he had doled her out a small allowance of pocket money ; how she had ascribed the dreariness of her life to his desire to save expenditure, and, behold, he threw a gift worth thousands into her lap as carelessly as if it had been a handful of summer blossoms.

‘ When shall I wear these diamonds ?’ she asked herself—or rather inquired of destiny—as she clasped the necklace around her throat before the glass in her dressing-room. ‘ Perhaps, if Sir Aubrey is inclined to be indulgent, he will take me to London this year, and let me be presented, and see the world. It is hard to have wealth, and jewels, and a title, and youth, and good looks, and yet to be buried alive at Perriam Place.'

The next day was the brightest of the new year, but Sir Aubrey protested against the yellow chariot when Mr. Stimpson, who was still in attendance, recommended a quiet drive.

'I detest being shut up in a coach,' he said. 'I'd rather take a little walk in the garden with Lady Perriam.'

'So be it, then,' replied the doctor, who wished to make his regimen agreeable to so profitable a patient. 'I don't know that a walk mightn't be better than a drive. Only be sure you don't fatigue yourself. Just a gentle stroll up and down the terrace, in the sunshine, with Lady Perriam's arm for a support.'

It was about three o'clock in the afternoon when Sir Aubrey and his wife went out for this promenade. A bright, tranquil, spring-like afternoon, only the gentlest west wind faintly stirring the evergreens, a calm blue sky with fleecy clouds, and a gentle sunshine upon the landscape. There had been much rain lately, and the pastures looked emerald bright against the dark arable lands, while here and there the first tinge of green showed faintly on the southward-fronting hedgerows.

'A beautiful world, my dear,' said Sir Aubrey, as he surveyed the varied prospect. 'I have seen a good deal of it, but I have found nothing so good as Perriam.'

'Perriam is very nice,' replied Sylvia, meekly. 'But you will show me a little more of the world some day, won't you, Sir Aubrey?'

'Yes, my love, we will travel a little more by-and-by, when I am stronger. I wish your life to be happy. I fear you have had rather a dull winter. But then happily you are not used to society.'

'No,' answered Sylvia. 'Perhaps that's why I long for it more than other people.'

'True, the unknown is ever delightful. You remember what Pope says: "Man never is, but always to be blessed."'

'I hate Pope,' replied Sylvia impatiently, upon which Sir Aubrey gave her a brief lecture on the folly of hating a poet whose philosophy is as correct as his versification.

The effort appeared to exhaust him, for he drooped a little on his second perambulation of the terrace.

'I am not so strong as I fancied myself this morning,' he said; 'I feel a little shaky in spite of the support of your arm. I'll go back to the house after this turn.'

They lingered a little for Sir Aubrey to rest on the spot where they had stood when he asked Sylvia to be his wife. Sir Aubrey looked down at the little green churchyard with a dreamy gaze. The very spirit of tranquillity pervaded the scene. The gray old church-tower, with its quaint corbels and water-spouts and varied tints of moss and lichen, stood out clearly defined against the clear cold sky. Death wore its softest aspect in that placid valley.

Mild as the atmosphere was the invalid shivered.

'I'll go indoors, my love,' he said; 'I am not strong enough for walking yet.'

They went back to the house, Sir Aubrey leaning a little on Sylvia's arm, and sighing once or twice during the journey, as if it were rather a troublesome business. The invalid returned to his easy chair by the fire in the saloon, where Sylvia gave him his book, a volume of the 'Spectator,' whose leaves he turned listlessly now and then, reading a page here and there, and smiling faintly at the familiar passages, or murmuring a quotation at the head of an essay. She arranged the little table by his chair, on which he kept a book or two, the day's newspapers, and a glass of weak sherry and water, and then prepared to take her place on the opposite side of the hearth, where it was her wont to beguile the slow hours with fancy work. Novels, and, indeed, modern light literature of all kinds, Sir Aubrey set his face against; thus woman's favourite amusement was, in a manner, forbidden to Lady Perriam.

But the baronet begged his wife to enjoy the afternoon sunshine. 'Finish your walk, my dear,' he said graciously; ' you can come back to me when you are tired of the terrace. I am always glad to have you near me, but you have been too long a prisoner.'

Sylvia obeyed. She was very tired of that spacious saloon, with its unchanging splendour—chairs and tables always in the same positions—no variety, no look of life or movement. She was glad to be alone with her own thoughts, which of late had taken shapes that disturbed and perplexed her. Sir Aubrey's unsettled health gave rise to agitating conjectures. She knew very well that there was guilt in many of these meditations. But she had never acquired the habit of ruling her own thoughts; she let them drift as they would, and the image which oftenest filled her mind was the image of one whom it was the first duty of her life to forget.

She walked to and fro for about an hour, and was beginning to think of returning to her post by the fireside and her duties of nurse and **comforter,** when she **heard a** distant step **on** the gravel walk, firm, light, and quick—a step that reminded her of Edmund Standen's. She **knew that the** step could hardly be his. **Mr. Standen's presence in that place** scarcely came within **the limits of the possible;** yet the sound **set her heart** beating vehemently, **so weak was** that undisciplined heart.

She walked towards the other end of the terrace, **and saw the well-known figure of** Mr. **Bain, the lawyer. He had been away** from Monkhampton **for nearly a** month, in the south of France, with his **ailing wife, whom the doctors had ordered to the** shores **of** the Mediterranean as **her sole** chance of **surviving the** severe winter. Difficult **as it was for** Shadrach **Bain** to leave business, he had **performed** his duty as **a husband, escorted his** wife to Cannes, and stayed **with** her until her health had been **in** some measure re-established. Monkhampton **had** been loud in **its** praises for this domestic **loyalty, though** some among his clients had grumbled **a** little **at the loss of their** astute adviser.

It had been no small relief to Sylvia to escape the **searching gaze** of those keen **eyes. From the very** beginning of her acquaintance **with Shadrach** Bain **Sylvia had felt that** here was a man who was in the habit of looking deeper than the surface of things, and that she had need to guard her secret thoughts against his watchfulness. He had always been courteous to her—nay, had evinced the most profound respect by his every word and action. Yet, knowing no more of him than that he was a good man of business, and a trusted agent of Sir Aubrey's, she felt an undefinable fear of his influence. Or, in a word, she fancied that he knew her.

He approached her with his usual grave politeness —not ceremonious—but gravely respectful.

'Good afternoon, Lady Perriam. I have just been with Sir Aubrey. He has been kind enough to ask me to stay to dinner—and as the dew is falling, he suggested that I should request you to come indoors.'

'There is no dew yet awhile,' answered Sylvia, somewhat impatiently. Sir Aubrey had a tiresome way of ordering her about through the medium of Mr. Bain. 'I shall walk a little longer.'

'May I be your companion during that time?' asked Mr. Bain.

'I have no objection,' replied Sylvia, coldly. She would have given a great deal to keep Mr. Bain for ever outside the gates of Perriam—yet, subservient

as he appeared, she felt that he was just the kind of
man to make her pay dearly for incivility.

'Your permission sounds almost like an interdict,'
said the agent, 'yet I will venture to remain. Sir
Aubrey must have been very ill while I was in
France.'

'Not worse than he has been several times this
winter.'

'Indeed. Yet I see so marked a change in him.
I don't know how to describe it, but it struck me at
the first glance, and I was pained to perceive it.'

'Do you think he is dangerously ill?' asked
Sylvia, turning upon him with a quick, bright light
in her eyes.

'No, Lady Perriam. I do not think there is
much danger of your being left a widow yet awhile,'
answered Mr. Bain, with inscrutable gravity.

'You really frightened me with your talk about a
change in Sir Aubrey. I can see no change myself
—and Mr. Stimpson says he is improving daily—
that there is nothing wanted but the warm weather
to make him quite well and strong again.'

'I am glad Mr. Stimpson is so hopeful. The
change which struck me so painfully was perhaps
more in Sir Aubrey's manner than his appearance—
there was an altered tone—a feebler manner—an

indecision about everything he said. I was talking to him nearly an hour about business, and I had plenty of time to observe him. In a word, he is not the man I left less than a month ago.'

Sylvia was silent. She remembered her own discovery of Sir Aubrey's uncertain memory—that almost childish habit of repeating his speeches. Did death begin his insidious work thus in the slow decline of the faculties? Sir Aubrey was by no means an old man. It was not time for memory to grow dim—for sight to fail—for hearing to grow faint.

'Let us go back to the house,' said Lady Perriam. 'If once Sir Aubrey gets that idea of dew into his head, he will fidget himself till I am indoors.'

'You have reason to be proud of such thoughtfulness on his part,' remarked Mr. Bain.

'Yes, it's very kind—but rather tiresome,' returned Sylvia, who was more candid with Mr. Bain in trifles than with other people—having that inward conviction that he could see through small artifices.

She went back to the saloon before going upstairs to dress for dinner—went back dutifully, to see if her husband had any further need of her attendance. Though there had been still a soft gray light in the garden, here in the saloon reigned deepest dusk, so much of the waning day was excluded by the draperies of those seven tall windows. The seven windows looked white and wan in the twilight, like seven tall ghosts. The fire had burned low, and only shed a ruddy glow upon the hearth.

Lady Perriam stood by the door looking in, Mr. Bain standing just behind her. Sir Aubrey sat with his arm hanging loosely across the arm of the chair, his head lying back against the cushions, an open book at his feet. He had fallen asleep, no doubt.

'I won't disturb him,' said Sylvia. 'Mr. Stimpson said rest was of great importance.'

'I think I'd better replenish the fire,' suggested Mr. Bain. 'It will go out directly if it isn't attended to.'

He went softly towards the hearth, Sylvia still waiting near the door, to see if that replenishing of the fire would awaken Sir Aubrey.

Mr. Bain knelt down, and put a couple of dry logs gently on the ashes. The dry wood began to sputter and crackle immediately. An ornamental brass screen, wide and tall, guarded the invalid from those flying sparks of burning wood.

The recumbent figure never stirred. Mr. Bain,

still on his knees, looked round at his employer. The dry logs burst into a sudden blaze which lighted all the room, and shone full upon Sir Aubrey's face. One quick, startled look at that face, and the agent sprang to his feet, and pulled the bell rope till a loud peal sounded through the house. Then he bent over that motionless figure, loosened the neck-cloth, raised the head, all quietly enough, Lady Perriam looking on all the while, with terror in her colourless face. She had rushed to the hearth when Mr. Bain rang the bell.

'Do you think he is dead?' she asked, in an awful whisper.

'No, I can feel the beating of his heart. Send a messenger to Mr. Stimpson on the fastest horse in the stables,' continued Mr. Bain to the servant who appeared in answer to his loud summons. 'If Mr. Stimpson is out when he gets to Monkhampton, let him fetch Dr. Cardross—if he's out, let him go on to Mr. Byfield. He must ride for his life, mind, and not lose a minute in getting off. And let another messenger—John Bates, he is a sharp fellow—go to Dr. Topsall, of Hedingham. Sir Aubrey has an attack—I fear paralysis. Tell some-one to fetch Chapelain.'

Chapelain, the valet, had heard that shrill peal of

the bell, and was by his master's side before the other servant had left the room. There was no time lost. Mr. Bain and the valet laid Sir Aubrey on a sofa, in the most comfortable position they could place him in, and this done, there was little more to do than wait the coming of medical aid. Perriam Place stood midway between Monkhampton and Hedingham. Either way the messenger would have three miles to ride, the doctor three miles to come.

' There's no hope of anything being here under an hour,' said Mr. Bain, who had been wonderfully self-possessed throughout.

Lady Perriam sat like a statue, hardly less white than the sculptor's marble. Her eyes alone moved, and they kept wandering restlessly from the prostrate form upon the sofa to the anxious faces of agent and valet.

' Is there any danger?' she asked, always refer-ring to that one, last, awful hazard of death. She had wished her husband dead, but the wish had been but a vague thought. She shrank appalled from the realization of that half-formed desire. There is something peculiarly awful in a wicked wish being gratified almost as soon as it is formed. It is like the direct interposition of Satan.

'A first attack is rarely fatal,' answered Mr. Bain, as calmly as if he had been a physician of long practice. 'There is every reason to hope that Sir Aubrey may be quite restored in a few days. But it is rather alarming while it lasts.'

'Alarming!' echoed Lady Perriam. 'It is horrible. Is he quite insensible, do you think?'

'I am not sure. He seems half asleep. I'm afraid this arm is paralyzed. It hangs so helplessly.'

'And is so cold,' said the valet, who was on his knees by the sofa, chafing the lifeless hand.

The dreary hour of waiting wore on, Sylvia sitting silent and unobtrusive, Mr. Bain and the valet doing what little they could, yet afraid to do much lest they should do the wrong thing. The ticking of the clock on the chimney-piece, the wood ashes falling lightly on the hearth, and Sir Aubrey's troubled breathing were the only sounds that broke the mournful silence.

By-and-by, after half an hour's waiting which had seemed half a day to the watchers, they were startled by feeble, half-articulate sounds. They came from the pale lips of Sir Aubrey, who was striving painfully for speech.

When he did speak, after that laborious effort, his

voice was dull and hollow. So might Lazarus have spoken when he came out of the cavern at his Master's bidding. To Sylvia those strange tones sounded like the voice of the re-arisen dead.

'Have I been asleep?' asked Sir Aubrey, in imperfectly formed syllables, as if in awful mockery of a child's first efforts to shape the words he hears from others.

'Yes, Sir Aubrey.'

'Very long?'

'For some time.'

The dim gray eyes looked wonderingly about.

'Why, is it dark already? Why don't they light the lamps?'

'We thought this subdued light was better for you, Sir Aubrey.'

'Better for me! I'm not an invalid—I don't mean to be an invalid any more,' mumbled the baronet, always with the same effort, the same uncertain articulation.

They did their best to prevent his talking much, or exciting himself; but, in trying to raise himself presently, he discovered that one side of his body was immovable; the left leg as well as the left arm appearing powerless.

'What is this?' he asked, more distinctly than

he had spoken before, as if terror gave force to his accents. 'I can't move; I've lost the use of one side. What does it mean?'

Neither the agent nor the valet answered this anxious question. They looked at each other doubtfully. The valet murmured some soothing speech in his own tongue.

'I know what it means,' said Sir Aubrey; 'it is paralysis, the one disease I have dreaded ever since I saw my grandfather wheeled about Perriam in a Bath chair, with his head hanging on one side, when I was a little boy. And yet I hardly thought it would seize me. I thought Mordred might be stricken; he has always been a weak, ailing creature. I never thought I should be the one.'

CHAPTER XIII.

MR. STIMPSON came in a little less than an hour from the time when the messenger started in quest of him. The man had found him at home, and the old surgeon had driven over to Perriam as fast as a good horse and a light gig would take him. He made his examination, ordered the invalid to be taken up to his bedroom, and suggested an immediate telegram to a famous London physician.

'We must have Crow down to-morrow,' he said confidentially to Mr. Bain, when he had assisted at Sir Aubrey's removal, and seen him made comfortable in the vast four-post bed, which had the grandeur and funereal gloom of a catafalque. 'The case is serious, and we must have a good nurse,' he added, in a louder tone.

Lady Perriam, Mr. Bain, and the doctor were all in the dressing-room adjoining Sir Aubrey's bed-chamber.

'Cannot I nurse my husband?' asked Sylvia. 'He likes me to be with him.'

'As his companion, no doubt—but to attempt anything more in his present state would be to impair your own health. We must get some reliable person to be in constant attendance upon Sir Aubrey. His valet, of course, will be able to do a good deal —but a woman will be wanted as well. I know what ordinary servants are; they soon get tired of sick-rooms.'

A curious look flashed into Lady Perriam's face. It had been cold and expressionless till this moment.

'I think I know of a person in London who would do,' she said, quickly.

'Has she had any experience as a sick nurse?'

'Oh yes—she has had experience. Shall I write to engage her?'

'It would be better to telegraph,' answered Mr. Stimpson. 'I can take the message, if you'll be so good as to write it.'

'No, I'd rather write to her. She'll want money for travelling expenses. I can enclose a bank-note in my letter.'

'Would it not be wiser to get some one from Monkhampton?' suggested Mr. Bain.

'I do not know any one in Monkhampton, and I

do know this person in London,' said Lady Perriam, looking at the doctor, and not at Mr. Bain. 'If my husband is to have a nurse, I should like her to be a nurse of my choice, rather than any one else's.'

This was her first defiance of Mr. Bain, and, trivial as the occasion seemed, Sylvia felt that it was not without its significance. She had an inward conviction that Shadrach Bain wanted to be master in that house ; aspired, in his presumption, to rule her even. Sir Aubrey's helplessness laid the household in a manner at the agent's feet. Now, therefore, was the time for her to assert her supremacy.

'I'll write to this person, Mr. Stimpson,' she added, without once looking at Mr. Bain, yet feeling that those cold gray eyes were watching her. 'You may consider that matter settled.'

'Very well, Lady Perriam. We must contrive to get on till she comes down. You are sure she is experienced ?'

'Quite sure. Do you suppose I would engage her if it were otherwise ?'

'Certainly not, Lady Perriam. Only your own experience of illness has been happily so slight. What is this woman's name, by the way ?'

'Carf—Carter,' replied Lady Perriam.

Mr. Bain observed the hesitation, and a bright red spot that kindled in the cheek of the speaker and slowly faded.

The feeble steps of shuffling, slipshod feet sounded without, the door opened, and Mordred Perriam came into the room, carrying an old-fashioned silver candlestick, with a guttering candle that had burned almost to the socket. It was one of the absent-minded bookworm's habits to let his candles burn down to the socket, and to let his fire go out half a dozen times a day. Custom had made him independent of servants, and he relighted his own fire, and had a stock of candles at hand to fill the empty candlesticks. No one ever gave less trouble in a household than harmless Mr. Perriam.

As he came into the dimly lighted room with the yellow glare of that flaming candle on his face, the same thought entered the minds of Sylvia and Mr. Bain. They were both alike impressed by the awful resemblance which Sir Aubrey's countenance, changed as it was by the paralytic stroke, bore to the face of his younger brother. That painful change which had aged the elder man by ten years made the brothers as much alike as if they had been twins.

Mordred stared at the three occupants of the

room in a helpless agitated way for a minute or so
before he spoke.

'Is there anything wrong?' he asked at last.
'Has anything happened? It's eight o'clock, and
the dinner-bell hasn't rung.'

'You had better dine in your own room to-night,
Mr. Perriam,' answered Shadrach Bain; 'your
brother is very ill.'

'Is he worse than he was this morning?'

'Much worse,' said Mr. Stimpson, and then he
told Mordred about the seizure.

'Why wasn't I sent for?' asked Mordred,
piteously.

'You would have done no good,' replied Mr. Bain,
with his practical air. 'Don't agitate yourself, Mr.
Perriam. Sir Aubrey will be all right in a day or
two, I daresay.'

'Is he in there?' inquired Mordred, pointing to
the open door of the bedroom.

'Yes, but you'd better not disturb him,' said the
doctor. 'Chapelain is with him, and he has fallen
into a doze. Quiet is a grand point—supreme quiet.
No one must go in and out but Lady Perriam.'

'Very well; I will do whatever is best, though I
should like to see him,' said Mr. Perriam, with
resignation, yet dolorously. 'But please don't keep

me away from him longer than is necessary. I am
very fond of my brother; indeed I have reason to be
so, for he is the only friend I have.'

Mr. Stimpson said something reassuring.

'Would there be any objection to my sitting here
for an hour or two?' inquired Mr. Perriam; 'I
shall not make any noise. I won't speak a word,
so I don't think I can disturb my poor brother. I
should like to feel that I was near him.'

'I see no objection,' said Mr. Stimpson, 'unless
Lady Perriam——' he added vaguely, appealing to
Sylvia.

'I have no objection to Mr. Perriam staying here,'
she said carelessly. She considered Mordred Perriam of little more importance than a piece of
animated furniture—wearisome on occasions, but
hardly worthy of consideration at any time. It
could matter very little whether he were in one
room or another. Mordred stayed, therefore, seated
in a warm chair by the hearth, rubbing his withered
old hands, and shivering a little now and then, or
occasionally breathing troubled sighs. Mr. Stimpson departed, after promising to telegraph to a
London physician directly he got back to Monkhampton, promising also to be at Perriam Place by
eight o'clock next morning. Mr. Bain went down-

stairs with the doctor, but declared his intention of remaining at Perriam till a late hour.

'I have no patients waiting for me,' he said, 'so I'll stay as long as I can, and see how Sir Aubrey goes on. You might call at my door as you go by, and tell my daughters what has happened, Stimpson. They might be alarmed if I were later than they expected.'

Mr. Stimpson promised to do his neighbour this kindness. Mr. Bain went into the dining-room, where all was laid ready for Sir Aubrey's small family. There were the three covers set forth with accustomed pomp, far apart on the Great Sahara of table-cloth. Mr. Bain rang the bell with an air of being quite at home.

'Bring me some dinner,' he said to the butler. 'And you'd better send a tray up to Lady Perriam's dressing-room. She won't come downstairs any more this evening, I daresay.'

Lady Perriam was in no humour for refreshment of a substantial character. She told the servant to bring her some tea and take the dinner-tray away.

She was writing a letter when the maid went in with the tea-things. Sir Aubrey's dressing-room opened out of the bedroom on one side, and on the other communicated with that narrow passage which led to Mordred's apartments. Lady Perriam's dressing-room was a small oak-panelled chamber on the other side of the bedroom, a chamber that in days gone by had been used as an oratory by a certain Lady Perriam of Roman Catholic faith and Jacobite leanings. It was a narrow slip of an apartment, with a small fireplace in one of the anglés, like those one sees in some of the closets at Hampton Court. Three dark blue oriental jars adorned the high narrow chimney-piece, a fine carving of the Perriam coat of arms stood boldly out upon the time-darkened panel above them. Sombre green damask curtains shrouded the one narrow window and its deep-cushioned window seat. The washstand and dressing-table, of darkest mahogany, were small and inconvenient. A Chippendale pembroke table, with the famous claw and ball feet, filled the centre of the room, a tall narrow wardrobe occupied the end wall, and, with a secretaire and two roomy old arm-chairs, completed the furniture of the apartment. Seen by the light of two tall candles Lady Perriam's dressing-room had a somewhat gloomy air. One might fancy one of the State prisons of the Tower—that room, for instance, where Sir Thomas Overbury was done to death— about as lively of aspect.

Sylvia was deeply absorbed in that letter, so deeply that she seemed hardly aware of the servant's entrance with the dainty little silver tea-tray, though the maid, perhaps out of kindly concern for her mistress, possibly out of curiosity, lingered a few minutes to stir the fire, and to draw those heavy curtains a little closer.

The letter ran thus :—

PERRIAM PLACE, near MONKHAMPTON,
March 9th.

Dear Mrs. Carford,

I find it in my power to provide at least a temporary home for you, if you are able to fulfil the duties which will be required of you in the position I can offer.   In your struggles to obtain a living you may have sometimes been employed as a sick nurse.   If that is the case, and you feel yourself able to nurse and wait upon an elderly gentleman who has just been rendered helpless by a paralytic stroke, I can engage you as an attendant upon my husband, Sir Aubrey Perriam.   But it must be understood if you come here that you will say nothing about your past life to any member of this household, and that you will keep the strictest silence upon anything you may happen to know about my father.   I offer you this opportunity out of compassion for your sad state, and hope you will give me no reason to repent my confidence.

I enclose a ten-pound note to enable you to provide yourself with decent clothes, and to pay your travelling expenses. Please to buy a ready-made outfit, and come by the first train that will bring you conveniently after your receipt of this letter.

If questioned as to your qualification as a sick nurse, you must reply that you have had ample experience, but you need give no details. When you arrive here you will inquire for Lady Perriam, and you will call yourself Mrs. Carter, as I imagine you would hardly like to be known by the name that belonged to you in better days.

Yours truly,

SYLVIA PERRIAM—late CAREW.

This letter addressed and sealed, Lady Perriam looked at her watch. There was just time for a groom to catch the Monkhampton post, which did not go out till half-past nine o'clock. It now wanted a quarter to nine. She rang, and gave the maid the letter, with strict orders that it should be taken to Monkhampton without a moment's delay. The maid promised obedience. This business despatched, Sylvia drew her chair to the fireside, and sat looking at the ruddy logs on the low hearth, and meditating on the step she had just taken.

' Have I done wisely, I wonder ? ' she asked herself. ' Surely a woman who has suffered what this poor creature has gone through must have learned to keep her own counsel. It is an act of charity to give her a good home, and the day may come when I shall have need of a friend.'

Sylvia had hardly thought of her sick husband while engaged in writing this letter. She rose presently, opened the door between the two rooms, and looked into the baronet's bed-chamber.

Sir Aubrey lay in a doze, the fitful firelight now shining on his pale, altered face, now sinking into shadow. Chapelain sat in a comfortable chair by the bed, reading the newspaper by the light of a shaded lamp, which was screened from the invalid by the heavy bed curtain. On the hearthrug crouched the figure of Mordred Perriam. He had crept in from Sir Aubrey's dressing-room, noiselessly as a dog, and had been permitted to remain, unnoticed and unreproved.

CHAPTER XIV.

DR. CROW, the London physician, appeared at Perriam in the dusk of the following afternoon. He was the great man for all patrician ailments, having as it were a divine right to cure the aristocracy, landed and commercial, the episcopacy, and the bench, or, if incurable, to usher them decorously across life's mystic threshold to the unseen land beyond it. He was a square-built, genial-looking gentleman, with an ample brow, a large massively moulded face, and dark eyes, whose lustre years of closest study and hardest work had not extinguished.

He had come more than two hundred miles to see Sir Aubrey, but a quarter of an hour in the sick-room, and ten minutes in consultation with Mr. Stimpson, comprised all the time that he devoted to the consideration of the case. What he said in those ten minutes no one knew but Mr. Stimpson. But as he retired from the dressing-room where that brief conference had been held, Lady Perriam emerged from the shadowy darkness of the corridor to intercept the great physician.

Dr. Crow gave a little surprised look at sight of so fair a creature in that gloomy old house, whose unbroken quiet had struck him as almost sepulchral.

'Is there any hope?' Sylvia asked eagerly.

The doctor replied dubiously, in those smooth placid tones which tell so little to the anxious ear.

'My dear young lady, I am not without hope that your father's life——'

'Husband's,' murmured Mr. Stimpson in the physician's ear.

Dr. Crow gave another surprised look, but went on unfalteringly.

'That your husband's life may be prolonged, perhaps for many years.'

'But will he get well again?'

'Nay, my dear madam, there is no reason that his bodily health should not improve, with careful nursing,' replied Mr. Crow.

'Will he recover his mind?' asked Sylvia with increasing anxiety. 'Will he be what he was at the beginning of the winter, what he was yesterday morning even?'

'Alas, madam, I fear never,' answered Dr. Crow,

with tones of profoundest regret. Long habit had taught him to speak of his patients as if each new sufferer had been his boyhood's playfellow, the bosom friend of his youth, the companion of his manhood, or a beloved and cherished brother. The tone was soothing, though conventional. Disconsolate widows sobbed upon Dr. Crow's shoulder, and forgot that he had not been the familiar friend of their departed ones. Hapless mothers pressed his kindly hand. And if the doctor was somewhat exaggerated in his expressions of regret, he had at least a tender heart, and compassion for all sufferers.

'What!' cried Sylvia, 'will he live on for years, to be a very old man perhaps, and remain always as he is now—without memory—saying the same words over and over again, unconscious of the repetition, at times hardly recognizing the most familiar faces? Will he be always like that?'

'Always is a long word, dear Lady Perriam,' answered the doctor; 'there may be some slight improvement. We will hope so. The medicines I have prescribed may have a better effect on the clouded brain than even I venture to hope. We are in the hands of Providence. But I will not conceal from you that Sir Arthur——'

'Aubrey,' whispered Mr. Stimpson.

'I cannot deny that Sir Aubrey's mind **has** received a severe shock, and I entertain little hope of his permanent recovery. The mind may in some measure **regain its tone, but there will be, I** apprehend, always a cloudiness, even a childishness of intellect for which, dear Lady Perriam, we must prepare ourselves. I have promised Mr. Stimpson to come down again in about **a** month's time, when I may be able to speak with greater certainty. **In the meantime we are quite** agreed as to the treatment. **And** whatever **regret** you may naturally feel at seeing your husband's impaired intellect, dear madam, you may yet console yourself with the thought that you have him still with you. He might have been taken away altogether, **and** think how much worse that would have **be en.'**

Sylvia was silent. **Dr.** Crow pressed her hand gently, and withdrew, escorted by **the** respectful Stimpson.

' What a lovely young woman !' said the physician **as** they went, with hushed footsteps, down the broad carpetless oak stairs. 'And how young ! Hardly twenty I should think.

' Not **twenty, I** believe,' answered Mr. Stimpson.

' She appears quite devoted to the poor old gentleman.'

' She ought to be devoted to him,' replied Mr.

Stimpson, who, with the county generally, disapproved of Sir Aubrey's marriage. ' She was only a parish schoolmaster's daughter. However,' he added, remembering his duty to his patron, ' I believe she's a very amiable person, and as you say, devoted to Sir Aubrey.'

' Quite a pleasing thing to see,' said Dr. Crow. ' Thanks, my dear sir, you are very good,' he added graciously, in acknowledgment of the neatly folded bank-note which Mr. Stimpson gently insinuated into his hand.

The yellow chariot had been sent to meet Dr. Crow at the Hedingham Station, and now waited to take him back there. That stately equipage had scarcely driven away with its distinguished occupant when a humbler vehicle, a shabby-looking fly, drove round the broad gravel sweep before Perriam Place.

Mr. Stimpson had lingered at the door to watch the great physician's departure. He now waited to see the new comer.

' The nurse, I suppose,' he said to himself.

The surgeon was right. A slender, pale-faced woman, alighted from the fly, and looked wistfully about, as if in quest of some one to whom to address herself. She saw Mr. Stimpson, and hesitated, doubtful whether he were a servant or a gentleman, and whether, in the latter case, she might venture to speak to him.

She was decently but suitably clad in an iron-gray linsey gown, a black shawl and bonnet; but, simple as these things were, they were worn with a neatness that was almost grace, and the stranger looked like a lady.

'A superior-looking person,' thought Mr. Stimpson, noting every detail with his observant eye.

He went forward as the flyman lifted down the stranger's poor little trunk, and relieved her from her evident embarrassment.

'You're the nurse Lady Perriam has sent for, I conclude?' he said.

'Yes, sir. Can I see Lady Perriam, if you please?'

'You shall see her presently. But I should like to have a few words with you first about the treatment, and so on. I am the family doctor.'

'I am quite at your service, sir.'

'Oh, you'd better get some refreshment first, and rest yourself a little. I can wait half an hour.'

'No, sir, I won't trouble you to wait. I am quite ready to receive your instructions.'

'So be it. I shan't be sorry to get home to dinner. Just step in here for a minute.'

Mr. Stimpson led the way into the dining-room, where the butler and his subordinate had just finished laying the table, for two only to-night. Sir Aubrey's accustomed place was a blank.

Here candles were lighted and a bright fire burning, and in this light the surgeon made a closer survey of the nurse's countenance.

Where had he seen a face which this recalled to him? He could not tell. Yet there was something in this care-worn visage curiously familiar.

'I hope you have had plenty of experience,' said Mr. Stimpson.

'I have had much experience of sickness, sir.'

'Have you ever been a hospital nurse?'

'No, sir.'

'Have you any certificates?'

'No, sir.'

'That's a pity. You come here, as it were, without a character, and the place you are to fill is an important one.'

'Lady Perriam knows me, sir. I should have thought that would have been sufficient. I am here as Lady Perriam's servant.'

'It is sufficient as to moral character. But Lady Perriam's approval is hardly a certificate of capacity. She is too inexperienced herself to know whether

you are capable of discharging the required
duties.'

'If you find me incapable, you can dismiss me,
sir,' answered the woman, with a tone in which
meekness was curiously mingled with a quiet firmness—a woman who might be 'equal to either fortune'—able to face ruin calmly.

'Of course,' returned Mr. Stimpson; 'but I
don't want to expose my patient to the hazard of an
incompetent nurse. Have you ever attended upon
a paralytic patient?'

'Yes, sir. I nursed an old gentleman so afflicted
for nearly six months.'

This was the truth. Even adversity's bitter school
had failed to make Mrs. Carford a liar.

'You could refer me to the friends of that patient,
I suppose?'

'If Lady Perriam should require such a reference,
sir, I am able to give it,' answered the woman with
dignity.

'Very well,' said Mr. Stimpson, 'then we can but
try you. I like your appearance. You seem to have
seen better days.'

The nurse let this suggestion pass unanswered.
She put in no claim to bygone gentility.

'What is your name, by the way?'

'Carter, sir.   Mrs. Carter.'

'Good.   I am Mr. Stimpson, of Monkhampton, Sir Aubrey's medical adviser for the last twenty years.   Now for your instructions.'

Mr. Stimpson gave his orders plainly and briefly, and was pleased with Mrs. Carter's intelligent manner of receiving these directions.

'Upon my word I think you'll do,' he said, kindly; 'and now I'm going home, and you'd better go and get something to eat.'

'I'd rather see Lady Perriam first, if you please, Mr. Stimpson.'

'Was there ever such a woman?   Do you never eat?   Well, you shall see your patroness.   James, send Lady Perriam's maid to ask if her mistress will see Mrs. Carter.'

Sylvia had risen to a height wherein she was not approachable without a certain amount of ceremony.

Mr. Stimpson drove away in his old-fashioned gig —a relic of that departed age in which it was the mark of respectability to keep a gig.   Mrs. Carter waited in the hall till the servant should return with Lady Perriam's commands.

A plainly dressed maid-servant came down, at once upper housemaid and body servant to Lady

Perriam, who had not been allowed **the luxury of a** handmaiden for her exclusive service.

'**My lady will see** you,' **she** said, and Mrs. Carter followed her up the dark old staircase, along a wide gallery that led **to Lady** Perriam's dressing-room.

Here the wood fire **and** lighted candles made the darkly panelled room almost bright. Lady Per- riam sat before the fire in her glossy gray silk dress; the sunny brown hair making **a** coronet **above the pale brow;** the hazel eyes dark with thought. **It was** a picture that sent a thrill to Mrs. Carter's **heart.** The room seemed splendid **to eyes** that had for many years looked only on poor and sordid **sur-** roundings.

Sylvia received the stranger as it behoved Lady Perriam **to receive a** dependant and inferior. She did not rise **from her arm-chair to** offer the traveller welcome, but looked **at** her with a deliberate scrutiny, anxious to see **whether her protégée's** appearance **were** likely to bring discredit **on herself.**

'I am glad you have come here without loss **of** time, Mrs. Carter,' she said, **with** a distant gracious- **ness** which did not invite **familiarity;** 'and **I** hope **you may** be able to make yourself comfortable **here.'**

' There is **no fear of that, Lady Perriam,**' answered

Mrs. Carter, in tones that faltered a little, though she tried to make them calm. 'It is quite sufficient happiness for me to be near you.'

'Apart from that source of happiness—which can count for very little, I should think, between people who are so strange to each other as you and I are—you will have, I trust, a comfortable home.'

Mrs. Carter was still standing. No word, no gesture of Lady Perriam's had invited her to be seated.

'The comforts of such a house as this are very new to me, madam. I shall know how to appreciate them,' she answered quietly. She had schooled herself to command her tones by this time, but tears glittered in the faded eyes—tears which she quietly brushed aside, and of which Lady Perriam appeared unconscious.

'And you will know how to keep your own secrets, I hope, and those of other people. You will be dumb about any facts in my father's life which, in your former acquaintance with him, may have come to your knowledge.'

'I am not likely to speak of your father, Lady Perriam.'

'I shall consider that a sacred promise on your part.'

'Let it be a promise—I shall not be tempted to break it.'

'Very well, I will trust to your honour. And now tell me if I did wrong in sending for you—in believing that you must have some experience of sickness.'

'You guessed rightly. In my struggles for a livelihood I have acted as sick nurse. Amongst other patients I had one afflicted with paralysis.'

'That is fortunate. Then I shall not feel I am doing wrong in trusting you to attend upon my husband. Bear in mind that you will have to please our doctor, Mr. Stimpson, as well as me.'

'I shall do my duty to the utmost of my power, Lady Perriam.'

'You will occupy a room on this floor, near Sir Aubrey's. It has been got ready for you, I believe. You will take all your meals there, alone, and will have no occasion to associate with the servants. Your duties will not oblige you to sit up at night unless Sir Aubrey should become worse than he is now; but you will hold yourself ready to attend him at any hour of the night should his valet call you.'

'I understand, madam. I am not afraid of work, or late hours. I can be satisfied with very little sleep '

'I am glad to find you have one of the qualifications of a good nurse. Now you had better go to your own room—stay, I'll order some refreshment for you,' added Lady Perriam, with her hand upon the bell.

'One moment, madam!' said Mrs. Carter, stopping her. 'I want to thank you for your goodness in remembering one so fallen—so wretched—in providing a home for the desolate. I had no opportunity to acknowledge the gifts you sent me, for I feared lest any letter from me might compromise you. But I felt your goodness not the less. And that in your exalted station, in a change of fortune wonderful enough to turn an older head than yours, you should remember my misery, pierces me to the heart. Ah! Lady Perriam, you can never know how deeply.'

Sylvia's eyes—those eyes so little given to weeping—were dimmed by the time the woman had done speaking. The lashes drooped on her cheek, as she lowered her eyelids, as if to hide those tears.

'You owe me no thanks,' she said, after a pause; 'I am very glad to be of some service to you. I regret that the circumstances of my life prevent me serving you in any other way than that which oppor-

tunity offers. In spite of what you call my exalted
position, I am by no means my own mistress.'

'I can fully understand that, madam. It is only
waifs and strays that are altogether free agents,' said
Mrs. Carter, bitterly. For her freedom had meant
solitude and semi-starvation.

'I am glad to serve you,' repeated Sylvia, 'and I
venture to hope that if I ever should need help of
any kind you will be my friend.'

'Yes, to the death!' answered the other with in-
tensity.

'That means an unscrupulous friend, does it
not?' asked Sylvia, musingly, looking down at the
fire. 'A friend who would not stick at trifles if an
unpleasant service were required?'

'It means devotion. You would not be likely to
ask anything that involved wrong-doing.'

'You had better not think too well of me. I
make no claim to be considered faultless.'

'No one is faultless, Lady Perriam, on this earth;
but I hope and believe that you are as good and
pure as humanity can be.'

Sylvia sighed, and was silent for a little while
before replying to this last speech of Mrs. Carter's.

'I am the creature of circumstances,' she said at
last. 'Women are too weak to rise above their

destiny. I am something of a fatalist, Mrs. Carter.'

' A dangerous doctrine, Lady Perriam.'

' Is it? I am sorry for that. But come, you have had nothing to eat or drink since your journey, have you ? '

' No; I was more anxious to see and thank you than to eat.'

Sylvia rang the bell, and the maid appeared. ' See that Mrs. Carter, Sir Aubrey's nurse, has dinner, or tea, or whatever she likes best in her own room,' said Lady Perriam. ' You remember the instructions I gave you this morning.'

' Yes, my lady; the room is ready, and I have taken in the tea-things and a dish of cold meat for Mrs. Carter.'

' You will give Mrs. Carter wine, or anything she pleases.'

' Thank you, Lady Perriam, but I take neither wine nor beer.'

' You are a teetotaler, perhaps ? '

' I have taken no pledge, but a nurse cannot keep her head too clear. I shall take nothing but tea and coffee while I am in your service.'

' That must be as you please. Good night.'

' Good night, madam.'

'You will begin your duties as soon as you have dined.'

'Yes, madam; Mr. Stimpson has told me all I have to do.'

Lady Perriam bent her head courteously as the new nurse retired.

Martha led the way to another door in the same gallery, and ushered Mrs. Carter into a comfortably furnished bedroom. A fire burned cheerily in the wide basket-shaped grate, and a round table, with a tea-tray and plates and dishes on spotless damask, had been drawn near the hearth. Such comfort, plain and unadorned as it was, struck Mrs. Carter deeply. When the servant had left her, she sat for a little while looking about her with wondering eyes. Such comfort seemed like a dream.

'Am I really to occupy such a house as this?' she thought, hardly able to believe in her exalted fortune; ' to live with my own daughter, and to see her every day; and yet never dare to open my arms and clasp her to my longing heart; to feel the words trembling on my lips, yet never dare to say, " Child, I am your mother!"'

CHAPTER XV.

WEEKS and months passed on, and Sir Aubrey Perriam's condition underwent little change either for better or worse. He had been struck down in the prime of life. He was now a helpless and, in all semblance, an aged man. His intellect, keen enough within its somewhat narrow range a few months ago, had now dwindled to the obscure and clouded mind of dotage. He was not mad: he had no wild delusions, no strange imaginings. The clouds that darkened his mind never opened to show him visions of the unreal. He held no mysterious converse with invisible interlocutors; he evoked no company of shadows out of the world of fancy. He was only a foolish old man, with a weak memory, and no interest in life, save in the most trifling details of his monotonous existence.

He, who had been formerly remarkable for the

polish of his placid manners, was now captious and irritable, selfish and exacting. Unconscious how much he was demanding, he would have kept his young wife a perpetual prisoner to the sick-room, and deprived her of all contact with the outer world, save during the hours when she walked slowly to and fro beside his invalid chair, upon the terrace above that peaceful hollow where the family vault awaited his coming.

Only by some exercise of diplomacy could Lady Perriam taste the joys of occasional liberty; but, as time wore on, she learnt how to manage her invalid husband, how to seem to comply without complying, how to avoid all hazard of irritating him, and yet have her own way. Mrs. Carter was of the utmost service to her in this matter, always able to smooth away difficulties, to appease the baronet's wrath when he was inclined to be angry—altogether an invaluable servant to Lady Perriam.

The nurse kept her solitary place apart from the household; rarely left her own or the invalid's room, save to take the air in attendance upon Sir Aubrey; held no converse with the other servants; scrupulously avoided all familiarity, yet was never uncivil.

The result of this uniform and blameless conduct

may be easily imagined. Not one of the Perriam
Place servants liked Mrs. Carter. She was pronounced proud, artful, secret; a person who, under
the smoothest outward semblance, concealed the
deepest and most dangerous designs. It was seen
by the servants that Lady Perriam took more notice
of Mrs. Carter than of any other dependant, and
this weighed heavily against the nurse. Sylvia could
hardly be said to be familiar even with Mrs. Carter,
but she was kinder and more gracious to her than
to any one else in the household, and the servants
talked of favouritism.

' I've served in this house, as girl and woman, for
nigh upon forty years,' said Mrs. Spicer, the housekeeper, ' and I've never yet set up for being a favourite. I make my courtesy to Sir Aubrey to-day if I
meets him anywheres, as humble as I made my
courtesy to him when I first come as a scullery maid,
a mere slip of a girl. But here is this Mrs. Carter
living upstairs in her own room, and having her meals
served up to her at her own table, and being waited
on by them as is good enough to sit down with her
any day in the week, I should hope.'

' I think she's seen better days though, Mrs.
Spicer,' said Mary Dawson, the upper housemaid;
' she has it in her looks and in her ways, somehow.

Her hands are as white as curd-soap, and as small as any lady's, and she has such a soft way of speaking; and I've seen her handwriting too—quite like a young lady at boarding school.'

'I suppose she's come over you with her quiet ways,' answered the housekeeper.

'No, she's no favourite of mine, she's so silent; and she must be proud, or she'd scarcely keep every one at a distance as she does; but she's always polite.'

'Too polite!' muttered Mrs. Spicer. 'She's like Lady Perriam herself. There's no getting at the bottom of her.'

'Do you know,' said Mary Dawson, 'I've sometimes thought that she's rather like Lady Perriam in the face, allowing for age and all that?'

'Allowing for a precious lot, I should think!' exclaimed Mrs. Spicer. 'There's not much likeness between that poor faded thing and Lady Perriam.'

Mary Dawson's suggestion was negatived by general consent. No one could see any likeness between the nurse and her mistress.

Sir Aubrey had been in his helpless, melancholy condition about four months, and it was warm summer once more, and the corn yellowing in the fertile fields between Hedingham and Perriam Place, when an event occurred which added considerably to Sylvia's importance, and made the future at once bright and smooth for her ambition.

The baronet's proudest hope was realized when he had lost all power to taste the sweetness of that once longed-for joy. His young wife bore him a son.

Merrily rang the chimes of Hedingham and Monkhampton, the one monotonous bell of Perriam Church clanging in amidst those sweeter peals, on the evening of the baby's birth—a glorious July evening, all the rich landscape and the distant ocean steeped in soft yellow light.

Edmund Standen heard those joy-bells as he smoked his after-dinner cigar, strolling about the garden with Esther and his mother—heard and wondered at the unaccustomed sound.

'What can they be all ringing for?' said Esther. 'It isn't the ringers' practising night. There go the Monkhampton bells as well as ours. Are the English fighting anywhere, and winning battles, Edmund? You know how little I read the newspapers.'

'No, Essie, England is honourably neutral just at present. Those joy-peals do not proclaim the triumph of our arms. Some victim at the hymeneal altar, I suppose.'

'They'd have rung this morning if it had been for a wedding,' replied Esther, who couldn't quite get over her wonder at those unusual joy-bells.

The old gardener, syringing an adjacent rose tree, touched his hat, and ventured to address the young lady of the house.

'Begging your pardon, Miss, I met Jim Baker, the under-gardener at the Place, as I was coming back from my tea, and he told me as Lady Perriam has got a son—born this afternoon. Mebbe it war for that the bells was ringing.'

'No doubt, Giles,' answered Esther, with a nervous look at Edmund. His cheek, browned healthily by many a ride to and fro between Dean House and the bank, and by many a run with the hounds last winter, paled at the mention of that too well remembered name.

Her son! And one of his brightest, sweetest day-dreams in his brief summer-time of love and hope had been a vision of the day when Sylvia's first child should be laid in his unaccustomed arms—Sylvia's child and his.

'Poor Sir Aubrey,' said Mrs. Standen, almost as if she read her son's thoughts on his clouded brow. 'He will have little pleasure in the birth of his son.'

The joy-bells rang on, and every note was bitterness to Edmund's heart.　He left the three ladies to
stroll up and down among the flower-beds, and went
for one of those long, solitary rambles with which it
was his wont to solace himself when the pangs of
memory were too sharp to be endured with a smiling
countenance, and that cheery, easy manner which
made him so dear to the household.　He had borne
his grief wonderfully, the women who loved him told
one another with thankful spirits.　He shared all
their small pleasures, was the best of sons, the most
indulgent of uncles, the most devoted of brothers.
He only who wore the shoe knew how it galled and
pinched.　Edmund Standen wore his shoe with so
good a grace that his womenkind fondly believed in
his cure.　The struggle had been sharp and short
they thought, and with one wrench he had plucked
Sylvia Carew out of his heart.　Were Sir Aubrey's
death to set her free to-morrow, she would hardly
win Edmund back again.　He knew her too well to
be again her victim.

Grief, like jealousy, is apt to make the meat it
feeds on.　Feeling the birth of Sir Aubrey's heir a
source of supremest bitterness, Edmund Standen
must needs bend his steps towards Perriam Place,
as if anxious to drain that bitter draught to the

dregs. He went across the well-known fields in the summer gloaming—bean-fields, where the perfumed blossoms seemed fittest abodes for elves and fairies—clover fields that looked darkly purple in the fading light—by wide stretches of feathery oats—by a bit of woodland where the thick fern filled the hollows, trembling like green water with every breeze—and so, as if summoned by that one monotonous bell, to the churchyard in the hollow, with its ivy-mantled stone wall—wall of mellowest grays and browns, with hart's-tongue ferns pushing their slender fronds out of every crevice.

The bell lapsed into silence as Edmund entered the little lane leading to the churchyard gate, a narrow lane with the wall on one side and a tall hedge on the other, a deep gulley between a green meadow and the rustic burial ground. People who live in the country are fond of churchyards, and God's acre seems a natural lounging place, a trysting spot for lovers, a playground for children, a tranquil scene where age may meditate upon life's brevity and the wide hopes beyond it.

Edmund went into the churchyard, climbed the low wall, and seated himself on the top of it. From this position he could survey the Italian garden and the south front of Perriam Place, whose lighted windows showed dimly in the summer dusk. He lighted his cigar. Let the smoker's disappointment be ever so bitter, he mechanically seeks consolation from tobacco. He sat smoking, and looking dreamily at those faintly shining windows.

'Is she happy, I wonder?' he mused; 'she has a new source of happiness—the mother's joy, which should be very deep. A new life begins for her from to-day; a new life in which self must needs be but secondary in all her thoughts. She will taste her child's innocent joys, suffer his baby sorrows, forget her own desires in his. And thus she will be further away from me than ever. Until to-day there may have been some faint regret for me still lingering in her heart; after to-day I shall be the most insignificant atom in creation in comparison with that new-born child. Happy privilege, to succeed to a new inheritance of hope, new capacities for joy.'

He thought, and with deepest compassion, of the afflicted husband and father, the clouded brain which this new light of home could hardly brighten. The particulars of Sir Aubrey's sad condition were tolerably well known in the neighbourhood. Mr. Stimpson, the surgeon, affected to be reserved upon this point, but by nods and frowns and shrugs, and confidential admissions to particular friends, had made the state of the case known far and wide. The servants also had tongues, and knew how to use them.

While Edmund Standen sat looking at the windows, and smoking, a man, who also had a cigar in his mouth, came with a brisk step along the terrace, and leaned with folded arms upon the stone balustrade, a few paces from the spot where Edmund was seated. In this new comer Mr. Standen recognized Mr. Bain, the solicitor, with whom he had frequent dealings in his professional capacity. Mr. Bain would as certainly recognize him. It was best therefore to accost the agent, Edmund thought ; lest there should appear anything surreptitious in his occupation of that particular spot.

'A nice evening for a country ramble, Mr. Bain,' he said, cheerfully.

'Bless me, is it you, Mr. Standen ?' exclaimed the agent. 'I shouldn't have expected to see you so far from Dean House after dinner.'

'That's because you don't know my habits. There's nothing I like better than an evening ramble, with no company except my cigar.'

'Isn't that a rather misanthropical turn of mind for so young a man as you are, Mr. Standen ?'

'I don't know about misanthropy—but I know

it's pleasant to be able to think one's own thoughts
now and then—instead of making conversation.'

'And you've chosen such a nice spot for your
evening's meditations,' replied Mr. Bain. 'Now I
suppose that old churchyard, lying under the shadow
of this terrace, with its balustrade and antique vases
and statues and so forth, is a scene which poets
and that sort of people would call romantic ?'

'I think one need hardly be a poet or a painter to
admire this old churchyard.'

'Really now ?' asked Mr. Bain, with an incredu-
lous air. 'You see it's out of my way as a man of
business. If I were owner of yonder house, I should
object to a burial ground so near my water supply.
I should fancy everything I ate and drank was
flavoured with the ashes of my ancestors. Have
you heard the bells ringing ?'

'It would be rather difficult to avoid hearing
them,' answered Edmund, with well assumed care-
lessness.

'This is a great day for Perriam,' said Mr. Bain,
between two puffs of his cigar.

'You consider the birth of an heir a great advantage ?'

'Yes, in this case, certainly. Sir Aubrey is only
tenant for life, and the estate would go to a far

distant cousin if he were to die childless. I know how anxiously he desired an heir?'

'Is he pleased at the accomplishment of his desire?'

'As pleased as he can be at anything, poor man.'

'His capacity for joy of any kind is limited, I imagine, from your tone.'

Mr. Bain sighed, and shook his head with a melancholy air.

'That's a subject I don't much care about discussing,' he replied, after a brief silence. 'Fortunately,' he added, with a keen glance at the young man's face, just visible to him in the twilight, 'whatever decay there may be in Sir Aubrey's mental state, his bodily health is remarkably good. Indeed, I shouldn't wonder if he were to live as long as you or I.'

'Starting with a considerable disadvantage,' said Edmund.

'Yes, but we live fast—wear our brains and fatigue our bodies to the utmost. He lives like a baby—neither thinks nor labours—sleeps as placidly as an infant in its cradle, and, as he has very little memory, lives almost without care. I see no reason why he should not live to be ninety.'

Not once did Edmund Standen inquire about

Lady Perriam. He knew not how near she might have been to the gates of death—knew not if her peril were ended. Was she not dead to him already? Could death remove her farther from him —or divide them more completely than her falsehood had divided them?

Yet he would have given much in that hour to know how she fared. It was only his fear of compromising her that prevented his questioning Mr. Bain as to her welfare.

He spoke a little of indifferent matters, finished his cigar, and wished the agent good night. Shadrach Bain leaning with folded arms upon the broad stone balustrade, watched the departing figure till it vanished in the narrow lane.

'This rather confirms my notion,' he said to himself; 'I thought there'd been something more than a passing flirtation between those two. Mr. Standen was deeply hit at any rate, though he contrives to carry it off pretty well. But she doesn't take matters quite so easily. The lightest mention of his name brings the blood into her cheek, and leaves it ashy pale a minute after. You'd better make haste and cure yourself of that fancy, Lady Perriam; for if ever you become a widow I don't think you'll find it to your advantage to marry Edmund Standen.'

CHAPTER XVI.

MR. BAIN MAKES HIMSELF USEFUL.

Sylvia's babe grew and flourished, and for the rest of that glorious summer time it seemed to her as if life had a new zest. The infant was such a novel plaything, and its existence gave her so much additional importance. The servants were more reverential than before. The mother of Perriam's future lord was a much grander person than Sir Aubrey's young wife. Sir Aubrey, being in a measure civilly dead, the household worshipped at the shrine of the heir, as if that unconscious infant were already master and ruler.

A motherly countrywoman, the childless widow of a small tenant farmer who had failed and gone to the dogs untimely, had been engaged as nurse. Mr. Bain, who knew everybody, had found this person, and brought her to Lady Perriam, with a recommendation so strong as to be almost a command. Sylvia would have rejected the woman, solely to resist an interference which she resented as a species of tyranny, but Sir Aubrey, who was present at the discussion, and who always sided with Shadrach Bain, insisted that Mrs. Tringfold should be engaged. Mrs. Tringfold was accordingly introduced into the household a few weeks before the birth of the heir.

Sir Aubrey forgot all about the business within an hour of the argument, but his influence had enabled Mr. Bain to have his own way, which Sylvia considered no small hardship.

'Why do you always take Mr. Bain's part against me?' she asked, when the steward had left them.

'Very sensible man is Bain, my love,' answered Sir Aubrey, in his senile way; 'can't do better than take Bain's advice. If Bain recommends the nurse, the nurse must be good.'

'I'd rather have chosen for myself,' said Sylvia, pouting.

'What can you know about servants, my dear? You're too young to decide properly. Very good servant is Bain—faithful servant.'

'Faithful to his own interests, I daresay,' muttered Sylvia.

Sylvia did not know that it was through Mr.

Bain's influence her future income had been made five thousand instead of two thousand a year; but perhaps even had she been aware of this important fact it would hardly have reconciled her to that ever watchful influence which she considered a kind of tyranny.

There was no one in that house, the mother not excepted, to whom that infant stranger seemed to give such heartfelt pleasure as to the sick nurse, Mrs. Carter. She deemed it her sweetest privilege to nurse him for an odd half hour, when Master Perriam's own special attendant, Mrs. Tringfold, was in an amiable humour, and disposed to permit such a liberty with her nursling. She hung over his cradle with a fondness which, if assumed, was the perfection of acting. The servants declared this show of affection was assumed, and condemned Mrs. Carter as a time-server and sycophant.

' She's always been able to get the blind side of my lady,' said Mrs. Spicer, the housekeeper, ' and she thinks she'll get more of a favourite than ever if she makes believe to worship that blessed child.'

Although this was the uncharitable opinion of the servants' hall, nothing could be more quiet and unobtrusive than Mrs. Carter's love for the infant. It was when she was left alone beside the cradle, or with the baby in her arms, that her soul overflowed, and she shed tears, the sacred tears of the repentant sinner, over that unconscious little one, or breathed a heartfelt prayer that his path might be far from the sin and misery that had beset her footsteps.

The time came, but too soon, when the charm of novelty wore off this last blessing, as it had worn off the splendour of her stately home, and Sylvia began to lose her first delight in the baby. He was a troublesome plaything at best, and if his mother allowed herself to take the sole charge of him for half an hour she was apt to find that half-hour the longest in the day. She was glad to hand him over to Mrs. Tringfold or Mrs. Carter, and to admire his infantine graces at a distance.

Sir Aubrey liked to have the babe paraded up and down his room now and then; seemed proud of him; and caressed him with a senile fondness occasionally; but at other times forgot his existence, and sometimes even moaned and bewailed his want of an heir. At first Mrs. Carter would bring him the child, and show him the folly of these complainings, when Providence had already blessed him with so fair a son. But after a little while she discovered how vain this was, and allowed him to utter his useless lamentations as often as he pleased, without endeavouring to demonstrate their foolishness. As time wore on, and the babe became advanced in months, Lady Perriam found him more and more troublesome. With every tooth he cut there was the same fuss and anxiety. He had innumerable small ailments, and peevish fits, and squalling fits, which Mrs. Tringfold put down to his teeth, until it seemed to Sylvia that he could scarcely have been worse if he had been afflicted with teeth sprouting out all over him like the almonds on a tipsy cake.

'I shall be fonder of him when he is a little older, I dare say,' the mother thought, self-excusingly, when she found the heir of Perriam more than usually troublesome.

So, little by little, as the months wore on, the child ceased to be the new delight and amusement of her life, and the burden of her monotonous existence weighed upon her as heavily as of old.

She was in some measure more free to do as she liked since Sir Aubrey's illness. He, who had been so completely her master, was now little more than a cipher in the house. Dead in life, he occupied a place upon this earth, yet was no more than a blank in the sum of its inhabitants.

Weary as Sylvia felt her attendance upon Sir

Aubrey, she contrived to be tolerably kind to him—schooled herself to a passive amiability which was the very reverse of her vivid nature. She read to him, and sang to him, and answered the same questions again and again with a patience which seemed almost sublime. But she restricted the performance of these duties to about two hours a day—an hour in the morning and an hour in the evening. More she declared would have killed her.

For the rest of his time Sir Aubrey was dependent upon Mordred Perriam, Mrs. Carter, and Jean Chapelain for society, cheered only by the doctor's daily visit, or by Mr. Bain, who came about twice a week, and went over the business of the estate with his employer as seriously as if the baronet had been in the fullest possession of his faculties.

Lady Perriam had now almost unlimited command of money. Sir Aubrey still kept his cheque book and signed all cheques for the maintenance of his household. He was quite conscious of each amount which he so dispensed at the moment, and invariably bewailed the largeness of the sum demanded from him; but his brain had lost the power to remember or multiply the figures of previous cheques, and he might have been induced to sign three or four for the same purpose and amount in one day, had his land steward asked him to do so. All cheques were written at the instigation of Shadrach Bain. He could alone obtain money from Sir Aubrey; and thus all sums required by Lady Perriam passed in a manner through the agent's hands.

Sylvia felt humiliated by Mr. Bain's mediation, but was fain to submit, for if she ventured to ask Sir Aubrey for money he always replied in the same manner. What could she want with so many cheques? She had plenty of gowns to wear; he was always seeing her in some new finery. She had a house to live in, and a carriage to ride in. What more could she require?

Sylvia would suggest that there were bills to be paid, and that some one must pay them.

'Let Bain bring me the bills and I will write the cheques,' was Sir Aubrey's invariable answer. 'Bain knows what I ought to pay. He is a sharp man of business, and won't see me imposed upon. You'd ruin me, Sylvia, if I allowed you to manage matters.'

Lady Perriam submitted therefore, and received all cheques from the hands of Shadrach Bain. He gave her ample funds to gratify her own caprices as well as to pay household bills. Sir Aubrey signed

a cheque for sundries about once a fortnight, and
sundries meant pocket money for Sylvia. She was
now able to gratify her taste for fashionable dresses,
rich laces, delicate-hued ribbons, at Mr. Ganzlein's.
She bought new books and new music without stint,
and crowded her dressing table with the latest
inventions in perfumery. She was able to send her
father a bank-note now and then, and to add an
occasional bonus to Mrs. Carter's liberal wages. If
the possession of money could have made Sylvia
Perriam happy, she might now have tasted the ful-
ness of joy. But, however pleasant it was to buy
fine dresses, it seemed a hardship not to be able to
wear them before admiring eyes. She might be
pleased with the reflection of her beauty when she
stood before her cheval glass dressed in the style
which Mr. Ganzlein assured her was the last
Parisian fashion, as worn by the Empress Eugenie.
But she turned away from the glass with a dismal
sigh, remembering that hardly any one but her sick
husband and Mr. Bain would be likely to behold
her splendour. Thus after a brief period of extravagance, she grew tired of buying fine dresses.

She might have gone to Hedingham Church every
Sunday, and shown off her finery among people who
had known her in her poverty, but this she did not

care to do. That one scornful look from **Edmund**
Standen had been almost more than she could bear.
She could **not** hazard its recurrence. Better never
to see his face again than to see it with that expression. Yet when she dreamed **of** the dim unknown
future—and all her dreams were of the future—she
did not despair **of winning** her forsaken lover **once
again, were she but free to attempt** the winning.

There was one person in **Perriam** Place in **whom**
Sir Aubrey's altered state had worked **a** change
almost as melancholy as the change in Sir Aubrey
himself. This was Mordred Perriam, who had taken
his brother's affliction deeply **to heart; so** deeply
that it seemed as if the very mainspring of his life
were broken and the vigour of **the** man so **wasted**
and decayed that in the dismal journey to the grave
the younger brother was likely to go before the elder.
Mordred made no formal complaint of illness, though
to any ear that would hearken he did occasionally
bewail those sharp, shooting pangs which afflicted
his internal being; now striking the heart, now
assailing the head. He shuffled about very much
as usual, and shambled up and down his accustomed
walks in the kitchen garden; but all his joy in life
seemed gone. **He** had never stirred out of his own
room since his brother's attack save **to go to**

Aubrey's room, or for his constitutional walk in the kitchen-garden. He couldn't bear the sight of the dining-room without Aubrey, he said; so, at his request, all his meals were taken to him in his own littered chamber, and he sat among his dingy brown-backed folios, and quartos, and octavos, and mumbled his solitary meal, indifferent, or hardly conscious what he ate.

He bought no more books; corresponded no more with second-hand booksellers; studied no more catalogues of book sales; and this in him meant the relinquishment in his share in life. Not Charles V., when he shut himself up in the Monastery of St. Just, could have made a more complete finish of his career than Mr. Perriam did when he closed his catalogue, and said, ' I will buy no more.' ' What's the use of my getting any more bargains?' he said, when Lady Perriam remarked on this change in her brother-in-law's habits, ' there's no one to sympathize with me. You don't care for old books. You like new novels, poor ephemeral things, which become waste paper six months after their publication. How can you appreciate an Aldine Cicero, in twenty folio volumes; or a Decameron, almost as rare as that famous edition which sold the other day for something like two thousand pounds? Aubrey could sympathize with **me**. Aubrey understood when I talked to him.'

Sylvia had in **some** measure merited the reproach implied in **this speech, for without being** absolutely uncivil **to her brother-in-law,** she had **let** him see her almost contemptuous **indifference to** his pursuits. She had yawned **when he showed her** some treasured volume; **and** she **had gone so far as to** show that **she** considered **book-bind**ing an ignoble **pursuit for a cadet of the house of** Perriam. From the first day of **his brother's** affliction Mordred Perriam seemed **to shrink away from Sylvia. He** recoiled **from that lovely butterfly-like creature, as if** the **very fact of** her beauty were **an** offence **against her husband. Sir Aubrey's** room was Mordred's **favourite habitation. To sit by** the fireplace in **winter** and summer with **his chair** close to the hearth, **even when the capacious grate was empty of fuel, formed** Mordred's **chief pleasure.** He brought a **pile of books with him every day, and would read aloud to Sir Aubrey when the invalid cared for that recreation, nothing discouraged,** though his brother made **the same imbecile** remarks day **after day,** and gave utterance to feeble criticisms **that went often wide of the text. He would make approving remarks on the piety of** Voltaire, **mistake**

Jeremy Taylor for Gibbon, confound Paradise Lost with Dante's Inferno, and in various ways betray the weakness of his decaying brain; but Mordred was happy if he would but appear to listen, and talk a little now and then, and seem content with his company. Thus day after day the two men sat together, both old before their time, both with the looks and the manners of men who had, as it were, outlived life itself, and now dwelt apart in a kind of hades, between the life past and the life to come.

Almost the only interest these two evinced in the actual world was their interest in the heir of Perriam. Of him, each seemed equally proud. The infant's presence always brought a smile to Sir Aubrey's wan face, a smile which seemed reflected in the countenance of his brother.

'Providence has been very good to you, Aubrey,' Mordred said very often in exactly the same complacent tone. 'It's a great blessing to see that fine little fellow, and to know that the Perriam estate need not go out of the direct line.'

CHAPTER XVII.

As summer changed to autumn, and autumn darkened into winter again, a gloomy shadow fell upon Mr. Bain's orderly home in High-street, Monkhampton, the forewarning shadow of death. Mrs. Bain, the gentle, thoughtful, managing house-mother, had surrendered the keys of store cupboards and china closets, wine cellar and cellaret; and there were those in the household who felt that she had relinquished them for the last time. Never more would she reign with unobtrusive sway in the narrow kingdom of home.

She had returned from Cannes at the end of April, wonderfully benefited by the milder climate of southern France. Her friends were loud in their congratulations. She had found a means of cure, or at least of permanent alleviation of her complaints. Asthma or bronchitis need trouble her no more. She had only to pack her trunks and depart like the swallows, save for that encumbrance of luggage, at the approach of winter. The doctor, Mr. Stimpson, agreed to this, with some faint reservation. It is not for a family doctor to damp his patient's spirits. There is your family doctor, sympathetic and pensive, who gazes at you with deploring eyes, and appears to think you on the verge of the grave; and there is also the cheerful and jocose family doctor, who talks loud even in sickrooms, and affects to believe there is hardly anything the matter with you. Mr. Stimpson was a cheerful doctor and a great favourite in Monkhampton. Unhappily, this particular winter came upon the world with hardly a note of warning, tripping up the heels of autumn as it were; and while people were congratulating one another on the fine bracing autumnal weather, the frost-fiend suddenly tweaked them by the nose, and fogs which, had they known their place, would have held themselves in reserve for the dark days before Christmas, enveloped the close of October with a chilly gloom.

Mrs. Bain was taken ill with her chronic asthma before October was ended, and Mr. Stimpson declared decisively that the intended emigration to Cannes was out of the question for some time to come.

'She couldn't bear the journey in her present state,' he said to Shadrach Bain, who seemed full of anxiety, though he said little about his fears; 'and by the time we get her round again, it may be too late in the year for her to travel.'

So, instead of departing to the pleasant shores of the Mediterranean, Mrs. Bain was confined to her own chamber, a large and comfortable apartment, overlooking the High-street, from whose windows, when she was well enough to sit up, the invalid could see all that constituted life in Monkhampton.

'It's better than going abroad to be away from you all,' Mrs. Bain said to her daughters, 'and we are in the Lord's hands all the same here as in a better climate. If it is his pleasure I shall get through the winter, Monkhampton won't kill me; and if it's his pleasure to take me, I shall be content to go. I feel myself a burden to your father, my dears. A sick wife is nothing but a burden.'

'You oughtn't to say such things, mother,' remonstrated Matilda Jane tearfully; 'I'm sure father does nothing but fret about you since you've been so ill. If you could see him as he sits at table, so full of thought and trouble, you'd know how he takes your illness to heart.'

'I do know that, my dear,' replied Mrs. Bain, to

whom her husband was chief among men, always just, always to be honoured, ' and that's why I feel it will be a blessing for you all when it pleases God to remove me. Your father will know that he has done his duty to me, and been the best of husbands, and he'll soon leave off fretting. People easily make up their minds to a loss when the thing has happened. It's beforehand they feel the most pain, while there's a little bit of hope mixed with their fears. No trouble that God ever calls upon us to suffer is half so bad to bear as we think it is beforehand.'

And then, with many pious maxims, and quotations from Holy Writ, words which came from the heart as well as from the lips, Mrs. Bain strove to console her daughters in advance for the loss which she felt very sure must ere long befall them. She was a woman of deep religious feeling, so thoroughly sincere and earnest that the formal phrases of Methodism had no sound of cant when she uttered them. It had been her greatest pride and her sweetest joy to bring up her children in the love and fear of the Lord. That sublime phrase was written on her heart, ' In the love and fear of the Lord.' And from no thought or action of her life was the influence of religion ever absent. Her simple, thrifty, unselfish life had been ruled on what she herself called gospel principles. She had been a bounteous friend to the poor of Monkhampton; a Dorcas in simplicity of living and attire—never choosing the best for herself—taking no more heed for her raiment than the lilies, and content with a homelier garb than that wherewith God decks the flowers of the field.

The only pang she had ever felt on her husband's account was the fear that he was somewhat given to worldliness. That, in spite of his regular attendance at the chapel in Water-lane, twice every Sabbath, and on two evenings in the week, the things of this world had too firm a hold upon his spirit—that his bank-book occupied almost as important a place in his thoughts as his Bible—willing though he seemed to read the morning and evening chapter.

' I could bear poverty better than the thought that your father cared too much for the things of this world,' Mrs. Bain said to one of her daughters plaintively.

The girl defended her father warmly.

' I think that is going a little too far, mother,' she answered. ' It's people's duty to get on in life, especially when they have families to provide for. I sometimes wish father was a little more worldly-minded, and would let us ride on horseback, as the Miss Horshaws do, and even follow the hounds.'

Mrs. Bain sighed, and murmured something about the incongruity of horsemanship and Biblical Christianity. She always came back to the Bible for strength in every argument; and in the Bible chariots and horses were generally associated with wickedness, and Egyptians and Philistines. She had done her utmost to teach her children how transitory were the joys of this life—and here was her Matilda Jane, her firstborn, hankering for horsemanship, and even eager to hunt some innocent animal to death.

No man could have been a better or kinder husband than Mr. Bain in this mournful winter, when the shadow of approaching death forbade all Christmas joys, and made the season doubly sad, because it had been wont to be enlivened by some mild domestic festivity, extra good dinners, a family gathering of all the Dawkers and Bains, and those other families with which Dawkers and Bains had intermingled in the solemn bonds of matrimony.

Every one in Monkhampton lauded Shadrach Bain's devotion to his sick wife. It was the habit of those simple townsfolk to survey and remark upon the actions of their neighbours as if all the houses had been verily of glass; and all Monkhampton agreed that in his character of husband Shadrach was a model for his fellow-townsmen. The Baptists said it was because Mr. Bain was a Baptist. The Church-of-Englanders declared that Bain was a good fellow in spite of his Methodistical nonsense.

It was known that he had been ready to take his wife to Cannes when her fatal illness came upon her; it was known that he spent his leisure evenings in her sick-room ; it was known that he had summoned Dr. Pollinktory from Rougemont, the county town, to hold a consultation with Mr. Stimpson, not once, but three times, since Mrs. Bain had kept her room. What could domestic affection do more than this ?

The twenty years which had gone by since his father's death had done much to strengthen Mr. Bain's standing in Monkhampton. A man cannot go on living in a substantial square-built house, paying his way, subscribing liberally to local charities, and bringing up sons and daughters, without winning the respect of his fellow-townsmen.

It was known that every year which came to an end beheld an increase in Mr. Bain's worldly goods. The addition to his possessions might be much or little ; but it was a well-known fact that Shadrach Bain saved money. He bought little odd bits of land here and there in obscure corners of the town —here half an acre and there a quarter, and here a dilapidated old house, only fit to be pulled down— until he had in a manner coiled himself in and out of the town like a serpent, so that no new street could have been planned in Monkhampton that would not cut through Shadrach Bain's property. Go to the right, or turn to the left, you must come upon some spot of earth that was the freehold of Shadrach Bain.

He had bought two or three speculative properties within the last year, perhaps hardly amounting altogether to three thousand pounds; yet it was an understood thing that he was getting rich, and that where in former years he had crept, he now began to stride.

A very dismal house was the habitation of the Bain family that winter. They all loved the mother, and to miss her quiet presence was to lose the keystone of the domestic arch. 'Father,' too, was beyond measure dull and self-absorbed. He rarely spoke to his daughters; he seemed unconscious of the existence of his sons, save in their capacity as his clerks, in which, to use their own unlicensed language, he was 'down upon them to an awful extent.' He worked in his office in all kinds of unlawful hours, and only entered the family dining-room to eat his unsocial and hurried meal, and to leave directly he had eaten.

The Perriam estate occupied him more closely than ever this winter, and two days in every week were spent at Perriam Place, or on the Perriam lands, riding the baronet's once cherished Splinter, which was kept in condition by Mr. Bain's occasional use. On these days he always took his luncheon at the Place, and sometimes shared that mid-day meal with the reluctant Lady Perriam. She felt that he was of use to her—that but for him her position would be a great deal worse than it was, and she schooled herself to be civil, friendly even in her manner to him. Yet, lurking in her heart, there was always the same un-defined fear of him, the same deep-rooted conviction that he knew her better than any one else in the world.

One day when they were seated at luncheon, far apart at the long dining-table, but alone and unat-tended, Mr. Bain spoke of Edmund Standen.

'A very fine young fellow that,' he said, 'and a first-rate man of business, which one would hardly have expected of a lad brought up at his mother's apron string. Edmund Standen would have come to the front if he had started in life without a six-pence.'

How deeply that phrase hit Sylvia, remembering as she did her own cowardly fears, her own weak shrinking from the mere possibility of misfortune!

'Standen is to be manager at the bank next year, I'm told, and Sanderson goes to Rougemont in the place of Mr. Curlew, who retires. He'll get six or seven hundred a year, no doubt, as manager. A nice thing, considering his mother's money, which must all come to him by-and-by. I suppose he'll marry that little girl he is so sweet upon.'

'Do you mean Miss Rochdale?' asked Sylvia, very pale, not knowing what he might tell her next.

'Yes, that's the name. The pretty little dark-eyed girl who lives with his mother.'

'They have been brought up together like brother and sister,' said Sylvia. 'They could hardly think of marrying, I should fancy.'

'Should you? It's the common talk that they're engaged. I used to meet them strolling in the lanes round Hedingham in the summer evenings; but perhaps it was only in brotherly and sisterly companionship.'

Sylvia answered not a word. What should she say? She had no desire to question Shadrach Bain. If this thing were true, the knowledge of it must reach her soon enough, too soon, let it come when it would. She shrank from receiving her death-blow through Mr. Bain.

'I could bear anything but that,' she thought, meaning Edmund's marriage with any one except herself. 'I could endure life-long separation from him, but not to know that he was happy with another.'

She could now venture to send for Mary Peter, the Hedingham dressmaker, without fear of reproof from Sir Aubrey, who need know nothing of that young person's coming. She summoned Mary on the day after this conversation with Mr. Bain, and received her in the morning room on the ground floor, that chilly apartment which the last Lady Perriam had adorned with a collection of shells and sea-weeds in two ebony cabinets, and a neat book-case, containing about two dozen of the dullest imaginable books. Here, remote from Sir Aubrey's ken, Sylvia could detain Miss Peter as long as she pleased.

'I want you to make a dress for me, Mary,' she said, with that lofty yet gracious air which became her as well as if she had been born in the purple. 'Sir Aubrey insisted upon my employing Mrs. Bowker, of Monkhampton, and I always defer to him even in small matters; but I like your style best, and I mean to employ you occasionally.'

'I'm sure you're very kind, my lady,' answered Mary, to whom the days when she and Sylvia had been companions seemed very far off, so vast was the distance between them now.

Then came a discussion about the fashion of the dress, and then the usual question, asked with a languid air, as if the inquiry were made rather out of civility to Miss Peter than from any interest Lady Perriam felt in the subject.

' Any news at Hedingham, Mary ?'

' Well, not much, my lady. You know there never is no news to speak of in our dreadful dull place. Mrs. Toynbee and the young ladies have been to Badden Badden, and only came back in November, with all the Parisian fashions—and very 'ideous the Parisian fashions must be judging from Mrs. Toynbee's bonnet, with not so much as an apology for a curtain, and flowers sprouting out where you'd least expect to see them. It would be worth your whiled coming over to church just to look at Mrs. Toynbee's bonnet, and one can see that she thinks a deal of it too. But you never come to our church now, my lady.'

' It's so far,' said Sylvia, 'I don't care about having the horses out on Sunday.'

' That's very good of you,' answered Mary wonderingly. 'I think if I had horses I should never have 'em in the stables, I should so enjoy riding about.'

'Is Mrs. Toynbee's bonnet the only event that has happened in Hedingham since the summer?' Sylvia asked languidly.

'Well, there isn't much else. There was a young gent from Oxford that stayed at the vicarage, and was thought to be courting the youngest Miss Vancourt, but he went away and nothing came of all the talk. Hedingham *is* such a place for talk. They do say Mr. Standen is going to marry Miss Rochdale.'

'I daresay that's true,' said Sylvia, steeling herself against the pain that went along with every thought of that bitter possibility.

'Well, I don't know, I'm sure,' replied Mary meditatively. 'It does seem rather likely though, as you say. Considering that he must have been so down-hearted at losing you, he couldn't better console himself than by marrying a nice young lady like Miss Rochdale; so kind as she's been to his sister's children too, like a second mother to them—teaching the little girls, and everythink, just as if she was no better than a nursery governess, instead of an independent young lady, with a nice income of her own.'

'Oh, no doubt she is a model of all virtues,' replied Sylvia, stung even by Mary Peter's praises of her rival. 'A young woman who knows how to wind herself into people's affections with her meek winning ways, and pretended unselfishness, yet seeking her own ends all the time. Just the kind of girl to succeed in any object she set her heart upon.'

Mary Peter felt the bitterness in this speech, and prudently refrained from any reply. She asked some convenient question about the sleeve of the new dress, and then retired. Sylvia would gladly have detained her, to question her more closely upon what rumour said of Edmund and Esther, but she felt that she had said too much already—perhaps almost betrayed herself to this vulgar dressmaker.

'I do believe she still cares for him,' Mary Peter said to herself as she went home with Sylvia's roll of silk under her arm. 'She'd hardly have flown out like that about Miss Rochdale if she didn't.'

CHAPTER XVIII.

SYLVIA ASKS A QUESTION.

THAT feeble lamp of life which burned in the sick chamber in High-street, Monkhampton, survived the gloom of deepest winter, now sinking almost to extinction, now flickering faintly back to life, now brightening so visibly that the anxious children began to hope for their mother's recovery. They might have her with them a few more years even yet, they thought. Early in February Mrs. Bain had improved so much as to come downstairs once more, and occupy her accustomed place by the household hearth; but she was not strong enough for the resumption of the domestic keys, or the economical housewife's duties. All she could do was to instil principles of thrift into Matilda Jane, to impart valuable secrets of good management, wise saws that had been handed down to her by her mother, look over the butcher's book now and then, and sigh plaintively as she noted how the weekly totals had risen since her illness.

'I told cook what you said, mother,' answered Matilda Jane. 'And she said it was the gravy-beef for your beef tea.'

'My dear, the bills could hardly have been heavier if she'd boiled down a bullock. I'm very much afraid the servants have been eating meat suppers.'

Delighted with this obvious improvement in his patient, and sincerely anxious to preserve the cherished wife for the anxious husband, whose devotion was a fact patent to all Monkhampton, Mr. Stimpson told Shadrach Bain that now was the time for his wife's removal to a milder climate.

'If you can get her out of the way of our east winds, we may have her strong again by the summer,' said Mr. Stimpson cheerily.

There was just a shade of uneasiness in Shadrach Bain's expression as he reflected on the doctor's suggestion.

'I thought our climate was pretty nearly as good a one as you could have,' he said. 'I didn't see much difference between Monkhampton and Cannes.'

'Perhaps not, my dear sir. In robust health like yours one is hardly conscious of change in temperature. Had you consulted the thermometer you would have found that Cannes is six or seven degrees higher than Monkhampton.'

'Very likely. If you think Mrs. Bain ought to go, she shall go, though it could hardly be more inconvenient than it is just now for me to take her. But she has been a good wife to me, and I wish to do my duty.'

'Everybody knows that,' replied the doctor with feeling. He had attended Shadrach Bain's family from the very beginning, had ushered the children upon the stage of life, and conducted them safely through all their infantile ailments, and was sincerely attached to the household.

'If she goes to Cannes and improves as you think she will, is there any hope of her being spared for some years to come?' asked the anxious husband, with a watchful eye upon the practitioner's countenance. 'I should like to know the truth. Patching a person up is one thing, and curing them is another. Have you any hope of a cure in this case?'

The doctor shook his head regretfully. Mrs. Bain had been one of his best patients—a small annuity to him for the last five years. Would that she could have lasted for ever, and been handed down in reversion to his sons.

'My dear Mr. Bain,' he said, overflowing with sympathy, 'your dear good lady's malady has long been chronic. There can be no such thing as cure, but by escaping our cold spring we may carry her safely into the summer.'

'To lose her when winter comes again. A poor hope at best.'

'We are in the hands of Providence. We can but do our uttermost. There is but one thing to be done, removal to a more congenial climate.'

'And that you consider essential?'

'Most decidedly.'

'Then it shall be done,' said Mr. Bain. 'However inconvenient, I'll take her over to Cannes myself. No one in Monkhampton shall be able to say I did less than my duty.'

'Bravely spoken, my dear sir. We all honour you for your devotion to your most estimable lady; a devotion equally creditable to you and its object,' said Mr. Stimpson, as if he had been making an after-dinner speech.

Mr. Bain, who held, like Macbeth, that whatever was well done when done, should be done quickly, announced his intention of starting with the invalid on the next day but one. The girls made haste to pack their mother's trunks, tearfully, yet not without hope. Cannes to their minds meant restoration to health. Matilda Jane was to stay at home and keep house, and rule the boys, a hardy race of grammar-school students with unappeasable appetites. Clara Louisa was to accompany her mother as nurse and companion.

'After all,' thought Mr. Bain, 'I don't see that anything can go wrong in my absence. Sir Aubrey is likely to hold out in his present condition for some time to come, and if there were any appearance of a change Chapelain would write me word of it.'

Chapelain, the valet, had a profound respect for the land steward, whom he regarded as actual master of Perriam Place. Sir Aubrey since his illness was but the shadow or eidolon of his former self. Lady Perriam had but little power, and what little she possessed she seemed to hold at the pleasure of Mr. Bain. The valet told himself, therefore, that Shadrach Bain was the idol before which he must bow down, if he desired his service to be a profitable one. Chapelain had reason to accord Mr. Bain even more subservience than is usually given by a time-serving domestic to the powers that be, for he was conscious of failings which, if once discovered by the steward, might lead to his swift doom and downfall. It may have been the joyless monotony of Perriam Place, or it may have been some inherent weakness in the man himself, but, whatever the cause, it is certain that since Sir Aubrey's illness Jean Chapelain had acquired the habit of taking more alcohol than was good for himself, or for the household in which he served. He had always liked his comfortable glass, but had kept the propensity tolerably well in check so long as he feared Sir Aubrey's scrutiny. But of late, since his master's eyes had grown dull and unseeing, Jean Chapelain had given the reins to his favourite vice, and had allowed that fatal charger to carry him very near the verge of ruin.

The Perriam cellars were too well guarded by the faithful white-headed old butler, who had held the keys for the last twenty years, for Mr. Chapelain to indulge his dangerous propensity at his master's cost. He had a certain allowance of beer and wine, and a liberal one; for servants, however faithful, are not apt to stint one another. They take a large view of servants' hall rations. But anything for which Mr. Chapelain craved beyond this ample allowance he had to provide for himself; and he did provide himself with some of the vilest brandy ever extracted from potatoes—brandy which was guiltless of grape juice, but which addled the valet's brain with a somewhat agreeable obfuscation, and took possession of his feet and legs, where it tortured him under the name of gout.

Little by little, tortured by the gout, and solaced by the brandy which produced the gout, Jean Chapelain fell away from his duties in Sir Aubrey's rooms.

The baronet, though apt to be peevish, and at times exacting, was not a very troublesome invalid, and there were few services he required which Mrs. Carter could not perform to his liking. He had taken a wonderful fancy to the sick nurse. Her quiet unobtrusive manner, her soft voice pleased him—even the subdued colour of her garments and her pale refined face were agreeable to him. Sometimes when his mind was a little weaker than usual he would mistake her for his wife, address her as Sylvia, and remain unconscious of his error till Lady Perriam entered the room, when he would look wonderingly from one to the other.

Thus it happened, the sick nurse being always on duty, that no one complained of Jean Chapelain's inattention. He dressed his master in the morning, but was very often out of the way when Sir Aubrey went to bed at night. On these occasions the gout furnished him with an ever ready excuse.

'My legs have martyrized me the evening,' he

would say to Mrs. Carter, in his curious English, ‘and I could not to descend. I hope the Old did not ask me.’

‘The Old’ was Mr. Chapelain’s name for Sir Aubrey.

Mr. Bain left Monkhampton with his wife and daughter about the middle of February—nearly a year after Sir Aubrey’s paralytic seizure, and about seven months after the birth of that baby heir, who had been baptized without pomp or splendour of any kind at the little church in the dell. At the baronet’s express desire, repeated many times, without variation, his infant son had been christened St. John Aubrey, the more surely to perpetuate that friendship which had obtained between Sir Aubrey’s ancestor and the brilliant statesman.

The child had grown and flourished in the dull old house, a vigorous sapling. The servants were never tired of praising him. He had Sir Aubrey’s blue eyes, or such eyes as Sir Aubrey’s had been when they too looked joyously and ignorantly on life’s glad morning. He had not inherited those wondrous hazel orbs of his mother’s, and indeed bore no resemblance to Sylvia, either in feature or expression.

That interview with Mary Peter had told Lady

Perriam very little about her lost lover, but when Miss Peter brought home the dress that had been entrusted to her for manufacture, the talk between the dressmaker and her patroness again fell upon Mr. Standen's affairs.

'I think it's a settled thing now, my lady,' Miss Peter remarked, as she tried on the dress, and settled a fold here, and pinched a trimming into place there.

'What is a settled thing?' asked Sylvia.

'Between Mr. Standen and Miss Rochdale. I met them out walking in Hedingham yesterday, quite like sweethearts.'

'How do you mean like sweethearts?'

'Well, I don't know. He had such an attentive way with him, and was carrying her waterproof. Besides it's in everybody's mouth at Hedingham. Alice Cook got it from her father, and her father had it from Mr. Vancourt himself, and he'd be likely to know.'

Sylvia said nothing, but suffered the business of trying on as quietly as if she had been a statue.

'They say it's to be in the spring, as soon as Mrs. Sargent leaves off crape. She'll have worn it more than a year and a half by that time.'

' Unfasten the dress,' said Sylvia, imperatively ;
' you've almost strangled me.'

Her breath came thick and fast, as if the dress
had indeed been tight enough to throttle her.

' Yet it isn't a bit tight about the throat,' said
Miss Peter, as she unfastened the body; 'twelve
inches—your old measure.'

After that day there came a restlessness upon
Lady Perriam which she strove in vain to conquer.
Were these two going to be married? That was the
question which tormented her, the question which
was perpetually repeating itself in her distracted
mind.   There were times when her own release
seemed so near, when she believed that Sir Aubrey's
sand ran low in the glass of Time.   Yet what avail
widowhood and liberty, if he whose love she counted
upon regaining were to wed another before the day
of her freedom.

She could not sit quietly at home to consider this
question, but ordered her carriage, and told the man
to drive to Cropley Common, a drive which must
take her past Dean House and through Hedingham.

Nurse Tringfold and the baby went with her, the
customary companions of her drives; but to-day
she took even less notice than usual of the infantile
St. John's endearing ways.   She wrapped herself in

her own thoughts, and sat looking out of the window with a gloomy brow.

They passed Dean House, but the untenanted windows looked blankly down at her, telling nothing of the interior. They drove through Hedingham without meeting a creature whom Sylvia knew, and thus on to Cropley Common, a wide waste of broken ground, clothed with furze and heather, commanding the distant sea, and far to the left the little sandy bay, and white walled town of Didmouth.

Here, even in winter, it was pleasant to walk on the close-cropped turf, though not on the loose ragged gravel road up which the horses struggled with their load. Half-way up the hill the coachman stopped at a bend of the road where there was a bit of a level which served as a landing stage for vehicles, and here Lady Perriam and the nurse alighted for a walk on the common.

To-day Sylvia—never fond of the nurse's company—was particularly indisposed to be social. She walked on rapidly, with her light footstep, winding in and out among the hillocks and furze bushes, and leaving nurse Tringfold in the distance, trying to pacify the complaining baby, who was afflicted by an obstinate bottom tooth.

How bare and desolate the landscape looked in

the bleak winter ! The day, which had been bright enough when they came, was now darkened by black watery clouds. Distant Didmouth gleamed whitely against a storm-charged sky. But Lady Perriam was singularly indifferent to that ominous darkening of the heavens. She had walked about half a mile away from nurse Tringfold and the carriage when she was awakened from her reverie by big drops of rain.

She had neither cloak nor umbrella, nor was there any nearer shelter than the carriage; not even a gipsy encampment or a hawker's cart within view.

Sylvia looked round her helplessly, not very much minding the rain, but with a sense of desolation at being thus alone and unprotected.

The sky had darkened almost to night. They had started for their drive directly after luncheon, yet it seemed evening already.

While she was thus looking round, a dark figure came between her and the sombre sky, a figure armed with that indispensable companion for a west country pedestrian, a large umbrella.

'Let me take you back to your carriage, Lady Perriam,' said the pedestrian. He was that one man whose voice Sir Aubrey's wife most feared, most longed to hear.

The sound of that voice coming suddenly upon her took her breath away. That Edmund Standen should speak to her at all seemed wonderful. To her mind—remembering that bitter look in the churchyard—it would have appeared more natural that he should pass her by and leave her to battle with the elements alone.

'You are very kind, Mr. Standen,' Lady Perriam answered with well assumed indifference. 'Yes, I shall be very grateful for the shelter of your umbrella. This kind of down-pour is rather over-whelming.'

Edmund Standen held his umbrella over her head, but did not offer her his arm. He had not desired such a meeting—nay, would gladly have avoided it; but he could hardly leave his sometime love to be half drowned on Cropley Common. There was nothing romantic in their encounter. Indeed that umbrella shared between them savoured of the ridiculous.

'Where did you leave your carriage, Lady Perriam?' asked Mr. Standen. He seemed to find a pleasure in giving her the benefit of her title.

'At the bend of the road, half way up the hill; I can hardly see my way back to it.'

'You may trust yourself to my guidance. I

know Cropley Common very well indeed. I often come here for a lonely ramble.'

After this he could hardly avoid offering Sylvia his arm. The ground was rugged, and slippery with the rain ; her feet stumbled now and then.

She felt that the time was short. If she wanted to resolve her doubts, she must speak quickly, no matter how abrupt her questioning might seem.

' I wonder you have any time for lonely rambles,' she said ; ' I hear you are very much occupied.'

' With the business of the bank? Yes, I work rather hard there sometimes. Fortunately for me, I like the work.'

' But I heard that you had another and pleasanter occupation for your time, in the society of a young lady to whom you are engaged to be married.'

' Pray who is that young lady ?' Edmund asked coolly.

' Miss Rochdale.'

' And from whom did you hear the report ?'

' From common rumour.'

' Common rumour is a common liar. I am not engaged to Miss Rochdale.'

' Nor likely to be ?'

' I will not say as much as that. There is no knowing when a man, who has missed his first chance of happiness, may seek a milder form of joy in a second venture. There is only one summer in a man's life, but autumn is sometimes a warm and genial season. There is that serene and beautiful autumn which is called an Indian summer. I may have my Indian summer yet.'

'With Miss Rochdale, I suppose,' said Sylvia.

'Why not with Miss Rochdale? She is a girl who might make any man's happiness, one would think—pretty, amiable, refined, intellectual, un-selfish. What more can a man ask for in the wife of his choice?'

'I see rumour has not been false, Mr. Standen.'

'Why do you trouble yourself about my fate now, Lady Perriam? It gave you very little concern a year and a half ago when you married Sir Aubrey. As you did not think about my happiness then, you need hardly consider it now. I live, you see; that is something. Here we are at your carriage.'

The footman opened the carriage door. Edmund saw the baby, splendid in purple and fine linen, fast asleep just now, and therefore a picture of infantine serenity. He touched the round, soft cheek gently with his finger, unseen by the mother, whose eyes, gloomy and despairing, were averted from him.

Lady Perriam hardly thanked Mr. Standen for the shelter of his umbrella, hardly replied to his courteous ' good evening,' and was driven away through rain and darkness with a gnawing pain at her heart.

CHAPTER XIX.

BEFORE leaving Monkhampton Mr. Bain had taken pains to impress upon his eldest son, a lad of sixteen, who had been exalted from a desk at the grammar school to a stool in his father's office, the necessity of keeping the absent head of the firm well acquainted with anything and everything that might happen at Perriam likely to affect his interests, were it ever so slightly.

' I don't see that anything can happen,' said Mr. Bain, after dwelling upon these instructions. ' Everything has gone on like clockwork at the Place ever since Sir Aubrey's illness, and nothing less than his death could throw things out of gear. But there's no such thing as certainty in life, and one can't be too much on one's guard. You must call twice a week at the Place while I'm away, see Lady Perriam, and hear how things are going on from her own lips.'

The youth shrank shyly from the idea of such temerity. He had seen Lady Perriam's yellow chariot before shop doors in the High-street, had beheld the lady herself come forth, beauteous and in splendid raiment, a being who scarcely seemed to tread the ground across which her graceful form passed. There was something appalling in the thought of making an uninvited morning call upon a divinity.

'Suppose Lady Perriam refuses to see me?' suggested the youth.

'She'll not refuse if you say that it was my wish you should see her.'

'I suppose she thinks a great deal of you, father,' said Dawker. The eldest son had been christened Dawker in compliment to his mother's family.

'I believe I have some influence with her,' replied Mr. Bain, with reserve.

'She's jolly handsome, isn't she?' exclaimed Dawker, betrayed by his enthusiasm.

'Jolly is not an adjective to be heard in a respectable household, Dawker,' Mr. Bain remarked, sternly. 'If I had said such a word in my father's presence, he'd have caned me.'

This was a favourite form of reproof with Shadrach Bain. His children had been brought up in a wholesome awe of those punishments which they had just escaped by a generation.

Having given his son detailed instructions as to what he was to do, Mr. Bain left Monkhampton almost easy in his mind. If what Dawker had to tell were unimportant, he was to communicate with his parent by letter, but if the news were vital he was to telegraph.

For three weeks Mr. Bain remained quietly at Cannes, watching Louisa's lamp of life faintly reviving, till it burned dimly, yet with daily increasing steadiness, or so it seemed to the husband.

' She will last another summer,' he said to himself, meditating upon this apparent return of strength. ' Strange how many false alarms we have had since her health first began to fail! How long the attenuated thread holds out!'

Dawker wrote to his father twice a week, like a dutiful son, and the head clerk wrote every other day, forwarding all important documents, or copies thereof, for his principal's perusal. Dawker's letters were as empty of intelligence as it was possible for letters to be. He told of his calls at Perriam Place, and how Lady Perriam had condescended to see him on every occasion, and had told him that Sir Aubrey's health was pretty much as usual. Dawker varied the wording occasionally, but the gist of his letter was always the same.

Three weeks at Cannes had more than exhausted the pleasures of that tranquil retreat. Perfect though Mr. Bain was in his capacity of husband, the monotony and seclusion of his wife's apartment wearied him, and now that Mrs. Bain was obviously better, he began to meditate immediate flight. His business was not one to be left long with impunity, he told the gentle Louisa.

' You'll have Clara Louisa to keep you company when I am gone,' said Shadrach; and Mrs. Bain submitted with all meekness to the loss of her husband's society as a melancholy necessity.

Mr. Bain, anxious as he had seemed to leave Cannes, did not go back to Monkhampton without loss of time by the way. He had heard a great deal about the delights of Paris, from fellow-towns-men more given to pleasure than himself; men who deemed a week's holiday in the gay French capital the crowning reward of a year's drudging amidst the dulness of a country town. Heretofore Mr. Bain had caught only flying glimpses of the wonderful city. But he was now determined to waste four or five days in tasting those enjoyments in the way of dinners, *cafés chantants*, circuses, and so on, which his Monkhampton acquaintances had dilated upon so rapturously. He wanted to see if to dine at a noted restaurant was really to rise to the level of the gods, he wanted to hear the Thérèse or Lolotte of the day—to see circuses which recalled the glories of Imperial Rome—to be able in a word to say, ' I too have lived.' He was a man who cared very little for pleasure, but he did not like being quite behind his neighbours in the knowledge of life.

So, without saying a word of his intention to Mrs. Bain, lest he should grieve that gentle soul by the idea that he could prefer the novel dissipations of the capital to her society, Shadrach left Cannes for Paris, meaning to put up at an hotel recommended to him by Tom Westropp, the auctioneer, one of the wildest spirits in Monkhampton. As he had said nothing of this Parisian holiday at Cannes, he meant to be equally reticent at Monkhampton ; or, if he alluded at all to his stay in Paris, he would put it down to the ever-convenient score, business. It was very easy to name some imaginary client as the person who had detained him.

Mr. Bain put up at the hotel so urgently recommended by Mr. Westropp. It turned out to be rather a dingy abode, not quite realizing the glowing picture presented by the auctioneer, who had, perhaps unconsciously, embellished the discourse of private life with the eloquence of the rostrum. The bed-chamber allotted to Mr. Bain was on the ground floor, abutting on a darksome courtyard. The coffee-room where Mr. Bain took his solitary breakfast of beefsteak and fried potatoes was not a lively apartment. Altogether Mr. Bain thought that he had seen many an English inn more attractive of aspect than this famous hostelry.

He took his fill of Parisian pleasures, saw all the horsemanship to be seen in the Champs Elysées, heard Thérèse and Lolotte, dined to his heart's content, and made himself bilious with new sauces and unaccustomed wines, and in four days had had as much of Parisian life as he cared about. He went home yearning for Monkhampton, his office, his iron safe, his letter book. After the bustle of that strange garish city his native town seemed to him the one delectable spot on earth.

His clerk's letters had been wholly satisfactory, so he went home without any feeling of uneasiness.

He had sent no intimation of return to his household, so that there was no dog-cart to meet him at the station when he arrived at Monkhampton, at about five o'clock in the afternoon, having been travelling since seven o'clock on the previous evening.

He left his bag and portmanteau to be sent after him, and walked quietly home, opened the door, and went in. The house had its accustomed orderly look, not a chair out of its place. Nothing could have gone wrong here, he thought.

It was tea time, always a comfortable hour in homely middle-class houses—an hour of rest and respite from the care and toil of the day. Mr. Bain went into the dining-room, which was cheerfully lighted with gas and a blazing fire. The healthy tribe of junior Bains was assembled round the capacious table, Matilda Jane ministering to their numerous wants. A substantial quartern loaf was succumbing beneath the slashing cuts of Humphrey, the second boy, while Maria, the third girl, was doling out a plain cake, a cake of such an unpretending nature that but for a few currants and a sprinkling of caraway seeds, it might have passed for bread. Dawker, a boy of luxurious habits, was kneeling before the fire, toasting muffins, bought with his own pocket money, muffins being luxuries which Mrs. Bain considered at once bilious and sinful.

Altogether there was an air of enjoyment in the party, which reminded Mr. Bain of a vulgar proverb about cats and mice, and he had a slightly offended feeling at seeing how comfortable his children could be without him.   There was more noise than there was wont to be in his presence, the gas was flaming higher, the fire burned like a furnace.

At sight of the head of the household all mirth ceased.   Every father of a family is more or less awful when he bursts upon the home circle without any note of warning.

'Good gracious, pa!' shrieked Matilda Jane, conscious of the open volume of a novel lurking beside the tea tray.   'What a start you did give me!'

'We've been expecting you every minute for the last four days,' said Dawker, laying down his toasting-fork in the fender, and abandoning his muffin to its fate.   'Didn't you get my telegram?'

'What telegram?' inquired Mr. Bain, uneasily.

'The one I sent to Cannes last Thursday.   I made sure you'd come back as fast as the trains and boat would carry you.'

Last Thursday—nearly a week ago.   This was Wednesday.

'What did you telegraph about, boy?'

'To tell you of Sir Aubrey's death.'

'Sir Aubrey's death!' echoed Shadrach Bain, aghast.   'Is Sir Aubrey Perriam dead?'

'Yes, father.   He died suddenly on Wednesday night.   We didn't hear of it till Thursday evening, only just in time to telegraph. The clerk said the telegram might not reach Cannes till Friday morning.'

Mr. Bain had left Cannes for Paris by the night mail on Thursday evening.

' We got a letter from Clara Louisa on Monday to say that you'd left, and would be at home before her letter. So when you didn't come home, we didn't know what to think had become of you.'

' You seem to have made yourself pretty comfortable under the circumstances,' said Mr. Bain, grimly. 'Sir Aubrey dead! I can hardly bring myself to believe it. Dead, and I out of the way when he died! I wouldn't have had it happen for a great deal. Dead—buried, I suppose.'

' Yes, father. The funeral was this morning—a very quiet funeral. I went over to have a look, though I wasn't asked. There were only Lady Perriam, Mr. Stimpson, and the servants, for mourners.'

'Mordred Perriam followed his brother to the grave, I suppose?'

' No, father. Mr. Perriam has kept his room ever since you've been away. He's been getting queerer and queerer for a long time people say, and now he's altogether gone—*non compos*.'

' People say! What people?'

' Well, the servants at the Place. I was up there yesterday afternoon, and had a longish talk with the housekeeper. I wanted to see Lady Perriam, you know, as it was your wish I should call upon her twice a week—but she hasn't seen any one except Mr. Stimpson and the clergyman since Sir Aubrey's death. But I saw Mrs. Spicer, and the old lady was uncommonly sociable, and told me a lot about Mr. Perriam and his queer ways. His brother's death has quite done for him, she says, and he won't look at anybody. Mrs. Carter, the nurse, has to wait upon him hand and foot, pretty much the same as she did upon Sir Aubrey.'

' Humph,' muttered the steward, ' that's easily seen through. Mrs. Carter knows when she has a good place, and doesn't want to lose it. Now Sir Aubrey's gone she'll pretend her services are wanted by his brother. Has the will been read yet?'

' No, father. Lady Perriam said it was to be kept for you to read when you came back.'

' Very considerate of Lady Perriam,' replied Mr. Bain. ' And now, Matilda Jane, if there's no cold meat in the house you'd better get me a chop—or a steak. I've had nothing since I breakfasted at a coffee-house near the London Bridge Terminus.'

Matilda Jane flew to obey her father's behest. A

sober quiet had descended upon the family circle. The more tender of the olive branches crammed their young mouths with plain cake, and stared open-eyed at the author of their being. Dawker, who, being in the transition period between boy and manhood, had an exaggerated sense of his own importance, sipped his tea with affected ease, and tried to look as if he was not afraid of his father.

Startling as was the news of Sir Aubrey Perriam's sudden death, Shadrach Bain seemed to take it with an admirable coolness. He took off his coat and wraps, settled himself in his arm-chair by the fire, and sat in meditative contemplation of the glowing coals, but with no shade of uneasiness upon his thoughtful brow. Sir Aubrey's death in no manner disarranged the plans which the land steward had made for his future life. On the contrary, it fitted in with them—it was one of the events in his programme—calculated upon ever so long ago. It had only come some years—say about ten years—before he expected it. One of the obstacles upon that broad high road, along which Mr. Bain designed to travel to the winning-post, had been removed.

About his late employer's will Mr. Bain felt no uneasiness. He had drawn up the document himself, a few months after Sir Aubrey's marriage ; and

he had no fear of the baronet having made any sub-
sequent will. He knew that he had to the last
enjoyed Sir Aubrey's fullest confidence, and that in
the decay of thought and memory the invalid had
leaned upon him as upon a crutch.

Thus there was nothing uncomfortable in Shadrach Bain's meditations as he sat by his warm
hearth while the disordered tea table was restored
to order, and cruet-frame and pickle-stand, beer jug
and decanter of sherry, were set forth on a spotless
table-cloth neatly laid across that end of the table
nearest to Mr. Bain's arm-chair.

Some natural sorrow he may have felt for the
death of the man who had been in some wise the
author of his fortunes ; but in Mr. Bain's practical
mind all undue lamenting for departed friends appeared at once foolish and morbid ; a diseased indulgence, an irrational sensibility. He would have a
band put upon his hat to-morrow, and by that outward mark of woe reduce his regret to a symbol.
That done, he would feel he had done his duty to
the dead.

Had the Perriam estate been about to pass to
Horace Perriam, the unknown heir-at-law, Mr. Bain
would have felt considerable uneasiness and uncertainty. The heir-at-law might have cherished parti-

cular views of his own about the property, and might have dismissed Mr. Bain from his stewardship: but Providence, ever kind to the Bain family, had been pleased to bless Sylvia Perriam with offspring, and the existence of that baby boy, still struggling with the advance guard of his teeth, made things very smooth for the land steward.

Well did he remember the making of Sir Aubrey's will—how just at the last he had ventured to suggest that there should be some trustee named, to protect the estate of the expected heir—or the portion of the heiress, should fate refuse to grant Sir Aubrey a son—in the event of the baronet's death before the child came of age.

Mr. Bain recalled Sir Aubrey's offended look as he said, 'I hope you don't consider me such a very old man that I cannot possibly live to see my children grow up.'

'No, indeed, Sir Aubrey, I am only anxious to provide for a remote contingency,' the steward had answered.

'You men of business are so tiresome. Very well, if I must appoint a trustee, put in your own name. It will do as well as any other.'

This happened to dovetail into a corner of Mr. Bain's phantasmal edifice—that airy erection—built

with profoundest calculation, which symbolized his
future.

He put his own name into the will as trustee and
joint executor with Lady Perriam. Beyond this
honourable distinction Sir Aubrey left him the sum
of one thousand pounds sterling, in acknowledgment
of his faithful services during a prolonged period.
It was no large reward for service so untiring, so
profitable to the employer; but Sir Aubrey did not
make the bequest without a mental wrench. He
did not like dividing his money after death; it
seemed almost as bad as parting with it during
his life.

Mr. Bain ate a well-cooked steak and a couple of
pickled walnuts with as good an appetite as if there
had been nothing on his mind. He liked this plain
English fare, this solid beef and bread, washed down
with amber-hued bitter beer, better than the familiar
kickshaws of the Maison Dorée or Philippe's. He
liked the sober comfort of his home, the deferential
companionship of his children, who worshipped him
as a superior being, and trembled at the creaking of
his boots. He liked the snug retirement of his
office, where he spent the rest of that evening, looking through the record of work that had been done
in his absence, and wasting some little time in

thinking how Lady Perriam would be affected by her widowhood.

'Will she try to lure Edmund Standen back to her?' he asked himself. And this time his brow was darkly clouded, as if his thoughts were full of gloom.

CHAPTER XX.

PERRIAM PLACE without Sir Aubrey looked exactly the same as it had looked beneath his quiet rule. Strange that in the many forms which our grief for the lost assume there is none harder to bear than this changelessness in inanimate things, this immutable aspect of rooms and corridors, which are just the same as when that missing footstep trod them. At Perriam there were few to lament deeply for the departed master. Unless it were in that closed and guarded chamber where Mordred Perriam languished under the care of the sick nurse, there was no such thing as passionate grief for the dead. The servants mourned him decently, shed occasional tears by way of tribute to his memory, sat late over their supper table, talking of his odd ways, and his small economies, against which they felt no resentment, while he had been liberal in the maintenance of kitchen and servants' hall, falling without question into the routine of his forefathers, and consented to pay for as many kilderkins of beer and as much butcher's meat as his ancestors had paid for before him. The servants lamented their lord with decent conventional grief, but were a good deal occupied with their own mourning, which was of the best, and furnished to them liberally. 'Lady Perriam has shown herself quite the lady in providing our black,' the housekeeper remarked to her subordinates.

Mr. Ganzlein had been given an open order to supply all things necessary, and his assistants came backwards and forwards with bombazine and coburg, and crape and parramatta, and there was a pleasant bustle of preparation in the housekeeper's room and still-room, where the maids sat by the fire running seams and stitching bodies, in an atmosphere odorous with glazed lining.

How did Lady Perriam take this awful change? That was a question which haply no one at the Place could answer. She spent all her time in seclusion, shutting her door against sympathy. The death chamber, and her old dressing-room, and indeed that end of the house where Sir Aubrey's rooms and Mr. Perriam's were situated, she avoided as if the dead had been stricken by some hideous pestilence, and even in his last icy sleep could

disseminate poison. She had ordered all her
belongings to be transferred to the Bolingbroke
Room, a handsome chamber with a bay window over
one end of the saloon. A smaller apartment, next
to this, Lady Perriam transformed into a boudoir,
and sent for a builder to cut a door of communication between the two rooms. On the other side of
the bed-chamber there was a door already provided,
opening into a fair-sized dressing-room. These
three rooms Lady Perriam brightened and embellished with not a few modern luxuries in the way
of furniture, ordered from the chief upholsterer
of Monkhampton. An ash-wood writing cabinet,
adorned with china plaques on which a modern
artist's facile brush had sketched graceful groups of
children at play in a landscape which changed with
the seasons. A pair of sofas, an easy-chair or two,
curtains of a pale apple-green, lined with the
faintest lilac. White sheepskin rugs, to lie here
and there like patches of snow upon the sombre
gloom of the carpets. A French clock, which might
have kept careless record of Time's steady march
for Sophie Arnoult or Marguerite Gauthier: a stand
for portfolios of engravings, a small bookcase filled
with choice editions of Lady Perriam's favourite
poets, bound in myrtle-green morocco.

The acquirement of these things had been the first use which Sylvia made of her liberty. A childish employment, perhaps, for the solemn days between her husband's death and burial; but the distraction served to keep dark thoughts at bay, and the Monkhampton upholsterer was the most discreet of men. The funeral had been entrusted to his care; and it was after arranging the details of that melancholy ceremonial that Lady Perriam gave Mr. Scruto the order for those little comforts which were needed to make the Bolingbroke suite habitable. Lady Perriam dwelt upon this point. She only wanted to make the rooms habitable.

'There is so little actual comfort in old-fashioned furniture,' she said. Mr. Scruto, with a natural prejudice against all furniture not supplied by himself, heartily assented to this proposition.

He sent in the goods for Lady Perriam's rooms under cover of the winter dusk, as stealthily as if they had been coffins; and the transformation of the apartments was made so quietly that the always-sitting Vehm Gericht in the servants' hall passed no vote of censure upon my lady's proceedings.

Mr. Bain looked round him with unmixed surprise when he was ushered into Lady Perriam's boudoir on the morning after his return. The change in

her surroundings struck him curiously. It was as
if some chrysalis of his acquaintance had suddenly
developed into a butterfly.

Those apple-green curtains of lustrous silken
damask, those snow-white rugs, so deep and soft
that he felt it a kind of sacrilege to tread upon
them, the ashwood bookcase and bureau on either
side of the fireplace gave a new character to the
room. The bureau was opened and littered with
papers; two or three volumes of the poets, in their
green and gold bindings, lay on the little rustic
table by Lady Perriam's chair. The mistress of
the luxurious chamber lolled in her low arm-chair,
her beauty enhanced and set off by the blackness of
her weeds.

Shadrach Bain halted in the middle of the room,
almost dazzled by this unexpected picture. She had
lost no time in gratifying her tastes, and had begun
to live immediately upon her husband's death,
thought the steward.

Lady Perriam received him graciously, but with a
certain distant manner which he felt was intended to
keep him farther from friendliness or familiarity
than he had been during Sir Aubrey's lifetime.
She begged him to be seated, but the chair to which
she pointed was remote from her own.

Mr. Bain expressed his regret for her loss, his sympathy with her grief. She listened gravely to his condolences, and thanked him for them, but she did not enter upon any exposition of her feelings. She allowed her sorrow to be taken for granted, symbolized by her widow's cap, as Mr. Bain's grief was symbolized by his hatband.

'I have not allowed the will to be read,' she said presently; 'I thought it only right that you should be the person to read it, as you were Sir Aubrey's agent and adviser.'

'Sir Aubrey honoured me with his confidence,' answered the steward; 'I trust I may be also favoured with yours. Left so young in a position of no little responsibility, you will need a faithful adviser.'

He was thinking how lovely she looked in that sombre dress, with the ruddy light of the fire playing among the red gold of her hair, reflecting itself in the deep hazel eyes, so dark, so inscrutable when she turned them upon him with their steady gaze. She was not afraid to look him in the face, even if she feared him. Whatever the peril that threatened her it was in her nature to meet it boldly.

'I am not particularly fond of advice, Mr. Bain,'

she said, ' and young as I am I feel quite capable of
treading any path I may choose for myself, without
leading-strings. But so long as you serve the
Perriam estate faithfully, you will find me ready
to place the fullest confidence in you—as my son's
land steward.'

Mr. Bain fully understood the meaning of this
speech. He was to be relegated to his proper position as collector of rents, and preparer of leases and
agreements, overlooker of improvements, and so on.
He was no longer to exercise an influence over the
life of Lady Perriam herself.

She felt no gratitude for the liberal supplies of
money which he had obtained for her, no gratitude
for the influence which had always been exerted in
her behalf. She took the first opportunity to eman-
cipate herself from the bondage of his interference.

There was a brief interval of silence, during
which Shadrach Bain sat looking at the carpet, with
a clouded brow. For once in his life the land
steward was taken thoroughly by surprise. He had
not expected Lady Perriam to take this decisive
tone, to assert her independence so boldly. He
thought the restraints of her married life had
schooled her into submission, and that, finding
herself suddenly standing alone in the world, on a

height that should have made her giddy, she would have naturally turned to him for counsel and assistance. He had done his uttermost to prove himself her friend; yet she now treated him as if he had shown himself her enemy.

'She is not a woman to be swayed by kindness,' he thought. 'She must be ruled with an iron hand. Easy enough to rule such a woman if one had but a hold upon her.'

'When do you propose to read the will, Mr. Bain?' Lady Perriam asked, after that pause in the conversation.

'Whenever it may be most convenient to yourself, Lady Perriam.'

'It cannot be too soon for me. I wish to know my exact position in this house.'

'I do not think there can be any doubt as to your position; nor do you seem to have entertained any uncertainty upon the subject,' said Mr. Bain, with a glance round the room.

'You allude to my additions to the furniture of this room,' returned Sylvia, interpreting the look. 'I can easily remove these things if I have no longer any right to inhabit Perriam.'

'There is no reason why I should affect a mystery upon the subject of Sir Aubrey's will, Lady Perriam.

The only will that I know him to have made was drawn up by me. It leaves you sole mistress of Perriam during your son's minority. Had you been a childless widow, you would have had only five thousand a year under your settlement, and three out of those five thousand you would have owed to my influence. Sir Aubrey proposed to settle only two thousand. But he was more liberal to the mother of his child than he was inclined to be to his wife, and your marriage settlement gives you the right to occupy Perriam Place during your son's minority. There is also an allowance of a thousand a year for your son's maintenance, provided for in the settlement. This, with the five thousand which is yours unconditionally, will give you six thousand per annum—an income which Sir Aubrey could not have given you had he not possessed large resources outside the Perriam estate proper. And I may venture to say, without presumption, that he owes much of that wealth to the careful management of my father and myself, during a period of half a century.'

Six thousand a year! A handsome income for the schoolmaster's daughter, who had so often sighed vainly for half-a-crown to buy a pair of gloves, for whom the middle-class comforts of genteel life at Hedingham had seemed as far off as the joys of

Paradise. Sylvia's countenance, which had worn an inscrutable look during this interview with Mr. Bain, changed ever so little at this announcement. The oval cheek grew paler than before, and a sudden light flashed into the hazel eyes. Transient was this indication of emotion. Nothing could be calmer than Lady Perriam's tone when she spoke.

'Sir Aubrey has been only too good to me,' she said. 'Can you read the will to-morrow morning? I daresay there are legacies to some of the old servants, and they will be anxious to learn their fates.'

'To-morrow at twelve o'clock, if you please, Lady Perriam. Will you go with me to Sir Aubrey's room to look for the will? I know where he kept it.' Lady Perriam's cheek, so pale a few moments ago, grew ashy white now.

'I have a horror of that room,' she said; 'but if you like I'll go with you,' nerving herself for the ordeal, and rising from her luxurious nest by the fire.

She took some keys from a drawer in the desk, and left the room, followed at a respectful distance by Shadrach Bain. They went along the west corridor, across an open landing at the top of the grand staircase, and into the east corridor, which led to Sir Aubrey's apartments. Sir Aubrey's no longer.

The door of the dressing-room, which the baronet had used as his sitting-room, was locked. There is something awful in those locked doors of deserted rooms which have lately been inhabited by the dead. Lady Perriam turned the key with a steady hand, and went in, followed by the steward.

The room had been cleaned and aired since Sir Aubrey's death, and all traces of his existence thrust away. The chairs were ranged against the wall, everything in its place, the window wide open to the bleak March sky, as if in obedience to that Jewish tradition which counsels the opening of casements to assist the escape of the departed soul.

The desk which Mr. Bain had to examine was not in the dressing-room. He opened the door of communication between the two rooms, but on the threshold of the bed-chamber Sylvia drew back with a scared look.

'Is it in there?' she asked, with a shuddering glance at the tall funereal bed—that bed which, at its best, had reminded her of a catafalque. The blinds were down, and the shadowy room made darker by the deep brown of the oak panelling. The wide and lofty fireplace looked like the entrance to a cavern.

'Come in, Lady Perriam,' said Mr. Bain, looking

back at her, wondering at this show of weakness in one who had seemed so firm. 'I want you to be present when I open Sir Aubrey's desk.'

She followed him into the room, shivering in spite of herself, and drew near the table on which the desk stood. It was close beside that awful bed.

'So, my lady,' thought Shadrach, noting her look of horror, 'I have found out your weak point, have I? This disinclination to be reminded of your husband's death looks like remorse for some wrong done to him during his life.'

He opened the desk with the key given him by Lady Perriam, found the will in a sealed envelope, endorsed, and bearing the date which Mr. Bain remembered as the date of its execution. He looked through the papers carefully, and found no other will, not so much as a codicil.

'And now, Lady Perriam,' said the steward, turning to her as he locked the desk, 'tell me a little about my kind employer's death. I have heard nothing yet beyond the one fact that we have lost him.'

'I can tell you little more, except that his death was sudden—awfully sudden. I went to his bedside and found him dead.'

'At what time?'

'A little after midnight.'

'You were up late that night, then?' said the steward wonderingly. Midnight was an unholy hour in the sight of the respectable inhabitants of Monkhampton.

'I am always late,' answered Lady Perriam. 'I am not a good sleeper, and sit up in my dressing-room reading. I had been reading rather later than usual that night, and went into Sir Aubrey's room to see that he was quiet and comfortable, as I always did, before I went to bed.'

'And you found him dead.'

'Yes. Pray don't ask me to enter into details. The shock was too dreadful to be forgotten. The horror of that moment haunts me day and night.'

'Is that why you have changed your rooms?' asked Mr. Bain. He was not afraid of questioning her now, not even of pressing home questions, now that he had found the weak spot in her armour.

'Yes, the association was too painful.'

'Was no one with Sir Aubrey at the time of his death?'

'No one. Mrs. Carter left him for the night about an hour before I went into the room.'

'Where was Chapelain?'

'He was suffering from an attack of the gout, and was confined to his room.'

'Did any one go for the doctor?'

'Yes; we gave the alarm at once, and one of the grooms went for Mr. Stimpson, who came before morning. He said Sir Aubrey's heart must have been affected.'

'There was no coroner's inquest?'

'No. Mr. Stimpson did not consider it a case for an inquest, though death came unexpectedly at last. Sir Aubrey had been so long ailing that it could hardly be considered a sudden death. Mr. Stimpson gave the proper notice to the registrar. He was very kind, and took all trouble off my hands.'

CHAPTER XXI.

'I DO BELIEVE YOU; AND I KNOW YOU TRUE.'

THE tidings of Sir Aubrey Perriam's death made a profound impression upon the people of Hedingham. They had been but rarely favoured with the sunshine of his countenance at the best of times, and for the last year he had never been seen beyond his own grounds, nay, his very existence had dwindled to a tradition. Yet now that he was really dead it seemed to the people of Hedingham as if a light had gone out; as if there were one star the less in their sky; as if things never again could be quite what they had been in the past.

Perriam Place abandoned to an infant, and a young widow of doubtful extraction. It seemed a disruption of social order. People speculated upon the life Lady Perriam would lead now that she was her own mistress.

'I dare say she'll give dinner parties after the

first year of her mourning,' said **Mrs. Toynbee,** who had not forgotten Sylvia's ungracious reception of her **only** visit.

'I should think she would **go up to London and** have her box at the opera, and **ride in Rotten Row,'** said Miss Toynbee. 'That's what I should do **if I were** a rich **young widow.'**

'**The question is whether she is rich,'** remarked Mrs. Toynbee, **with an** oracular air. '**We have heard** nothing about Sir **Aubrey's will yet.'**

'I suppose we shall hear of **it,' said the daughter,** with natural curiosity.

'I should think so. **Mr.** Vancourt is most likely to hear, and I dare say I shall be able to get it out of him. **And it will be** in the *Illustrated News* most likely after a week or **two.'**

Mr. Bain read the will at noon on the day after his interview with Sylvia, in the presence of **Lady** Perriam, Mr. Stimpson, **and** all the servants, **except** the two nurses, Mrs. Carter and Mrs. Tringfold, who **could not** possibly **be interested in a will** made **before their advent to** Perriam, and **Jean** Chapelain, who **had left Perriam** the day before the funeral, **to seek relief** from his chronic gout in his native southern France.

The reading took place in the dining-room—dreary

at the best of times, but more than usually dreary
to-day, when the nature of the ceremonial suggested
sad and gloomy thoughts. The servants sat in a
row against the wall, dressed in their new mourning,
guiltless of the slenderest thread of white to relieve
its dense blackness. Lady Perriam sat in an arm-
chair by the heaped-up fire, which was the only
cheerful thing in the room.

Sir Aubrey's will showed some thoughtfulness for
his dependants, though he had taken care not to
impoverish his personal estate by too liberal legacies.
He left small pensions to the older servants, and a
rather larger pension to Jean Chapelain, but pensions
which they were only to enjoy when superannuated.
To every servant who had been a member of his
household for the period of ten years he left fifty
pounds, to those who had served him over five years
he left five-and-twenty pounds, ' in recognition of the
merit of prolonged service,' said the will. There
was also a bequest of five-and-twenty guineas to Mr.
Stimpson for the purchase of a mourning ring.

To Mr. Shadrach Bain he left the sum of one
thousand pounds, to mark his high estimation of
services ably and conscientiously rendered during a
period of many years.

To his ' dear brother ' Mordred Perriam, Sir Aubrey

Perriam left his collection of gold and **silver snuff-boxes and** one thousand pounds, and he further desired that his widow or his children should continue to the said Mordred Perriam all advantages and privileges which **he** had hitherto enjoyed as an inmate of Perriam Place—that **he** should still occupy those rooms now tenanted **by him,** and reside at Perriam **free of all charge,** for the natural term of his life.

Finally, to his beloved wife Sylvia, **Sir Aubrey left all his** personal estate, which, with the income she would enjoy under her settlement, would amply provide for her maintenance. But in the event of his death happening before the majority of his eldest son, Sir Aubrey left his wife guardian of the infant, **with the privilege of** residing at Perriam during his minority.

Sir Aubrey's personalty included money in the funds, which would make a considerable addition to Sylvia's income.

The additional lands, tenements, **and heredita-**ments which had been acquired within **the** last fifty years, and constituted Sir Aubrey's independent estate, **were to be** equitably divided among his younger children, after the death of Lady Perriam, her interest in the estate under the settlement being only a life interest.

It will be seen, therefore, that the schoolmaster's daughter found herself handsomely provided for in her widowhood.

Rumour was not slow to spread the contents of Sir Aubrey's will among the gossips of Monkhampton and Hedingham. Mr. Stimpson, who did not consider his devotion recompensed by the trumpery bequest of a mourning ring, took no pains to keep the particulars of the will secret. It was sure to be published in the newspapers by-and-by, and he might as well have the satisfaction of communicating the news to his patients. Thus it became known at Hedingham that the widowed Lady Perriam had inherited all Sir Aubrey's personal estate, which added about a thousand a year to her income under the settlement. This, exaggerated by rumour, soon swelled to ten, fifteen, or twenty thousand according to the fancy of the narrator.

Those who remembered Sylvia less than two years ago as the village schoolmaster's daughter, lifted up their hands and eyes, and marvelled at this wondrous turn in fortune's wheel.

At Dean House the news of Sir Aubrey's death was received almost in silence ; yet it was a shock to more than one member of Mrs. Standen's household.

To Mrs. Standen herself the event was most un-welcome. Fortune could make no change in her dislike to, and distrust of, Sylvia. As Sir Aubrey Perriam's widow, with a large income, she was just as obnoxious to Edmund Standen's mother as she had been in the days of her obscurity.

Nor was this all. Though nothing definite had ever been said by her son, Mrs. Standen had of late been cheered by the hope that he would find a cure for his wounded heart in Esther's calm affection. He had breathed no lover's prayer in the girl's willing ear; he had made no promise to his mother. But he had seemed tranquil, if not happy, in Esther's society; and there had been something more distant and yet more tender in his tone and manner of late than the easy familiarity of an adopted brother. Esther and he had read the same books, and acquired a hundred fancies and predilections in common. They sang dreamy German duets, while Mrs. Standen dozed in her easy-chair by the fire, or worked at a lace-bedizened pinafore for one of the small grandchildren. It could hardly be possible to imagine a fairer picture of home than the family sitting-room at Dean House of an evening, after the seven o'clock dinner. The routine of busi-ness life, which kept Edmund away at the bank all day, rendered evening's repose doubly enjoyable. When he was an idle man he had been apt to tire of these simple pleasures, and had found evening in the family circle a long business. Now that he worked hard at his desk all day, he was bright and sociable in the evening, and never found the hours too long.

Was Sylvia's influence to spoil this tranquil gladness—to introduce discord once again between mother and son ?

Mrs. Standen trembled, but was silent. Esther felt that the new hope which she had cherished of late must speedily perish. What chance had she against that siren, whom Edmund had loved so passionately a year and a half ago, and perchance had never ceased to love. Esther knew that he had his hours of despondency, and she knew that despondency with him meant the memory of Sylvia.

However Sir Aubrey's death may have affected Edmund Standen himself, he heard of the event in silence, and with an unchanged countenance. He heard plenty of gossip about the event at the bank—gossip which for the most part took the form of speculation upon the value of Sir Aubrey's estate; but he said nothing. At home he was equally silent; even when thoughtless Ellen Sargent broke out with some ill-advised remark about Lady Perriam in the middle of dinner. Esther had but one thought—a thought which was almost conviction. Edmund's unextinguished passion would flame out once more, and while Sylvia's widowhood was yet new he would claim the old broken promise. Her treachery would be forgotten, or at least forgiven. He would remember only that she was free and that he might win her.

Esther was prepared to see the first sign of Edmund's return to the old allegiance in an altered manner to herself. He would be colder, more distant, unconsciously withdraw himself from that intimacy which had been so sweet to her, and had seemed so pleasant to him.

To Miss Rochdale's surprise, however, there was no such alteration in Edmund's manner. If he changed at all after Sir Aubrey's death, it was to grow kinder, warmer even. They were more than ever united by their mutual love of literature and music. They read Schiller together, to the secret disgust of Mrs. Standen and Ellen, to whose ears the gutturals of that grand Sclavonic tongue were unutterably barbarous. As the evenings lengthened, Edmund pleaded for after-dinner rambles in the meadows, where primroses and violets heralded spring's

carnival of field flowers. Mrs. Standen never went
out after dinner; Mrs. Sargent preferred the nursery
to any spot upon earth, at her little ones' bedtime;
so Edmund's natural companion was Esther Rochdale. She was too pure to affect prudishness. She
accompanied him for his evening walks as readily
and unquestioningly as if they had been brother
students at Heidelberg.

One calm April twilight—about six weeks after
Sir Aubrey's death—Edmund and Esther had strayed
as far as Cropley Common, that rugged heath upon
which Mr. Standen had met Sylvia in the rain-storm.
The hill-side, with its knolls and dells, and furze-
crowned peaks, wore a different aspect on this bright
April evening. The western sky was still warm
with the glow of sunset, and a waning moon shone
dimly in the vault above. The distant sea line was
purpled with the shadow of coming night, and one
lonely white-sailed bark glimmered far away upon
the darkening blue.

Edmund and Esther had been walking in silence
for some time, each wrapped in thought, when the
young man stopped, and proposed a few minutes'
rest before they struck into the homeward path.

Esther, generally ready to obey, on this occasion
demurred.

' It's late already, Edmund, and Auntie will be waiting for her tea.'

The superintendence of the tea table was one of Esther's evening duties.

' Let her enjoy rather a longer nap than usual, Essie. The sleep won't do my mother any harm, and I want to have a little talk with you.'

Esther complied, and seated herself on the grassy knoll which Edmund suggested as the best resting place. The evening—April on the threshold of May—was as warm as many nights in June.

' I don't see why we should sit here to talk, Edmund, since we have been talking more or less all the time we've been out, and are likely to go on talking all the way home.'

' Yes, I never find myself at a loss for something to talk about when I am with you, Essie. I suppose that means community of tastes, sympathy, and so on, eh ?'

' I suppose so.'

' Perhaps, after all, my real motive was a smoke. May I have a cigar ?'

' Of course you may. You know I am used to your smoking.'

' In that case I shall light up. These evening

walks wouldn't be half so nice if you objected to the cigar, Essie.'

'I dare say not. I think you would rather do without me than the cigar.'

'I don't quite know about that,' answered Edmund, gravely. 'I am very fond of the cigar, it is true, and if you forbade it I should feel the deprivation sorely. But I don't see my way to getting on without you. I never have been obliged to exist without you, you see, Essie. I can hardly judge what the flavour of life would be without Esther.'

Esther's lip, unused to express scorn, curled ever so slightly at this remark.

'You did without me very well when you were in love with Sylvia Carew,' she said. 'I doubt if you were conscious of my existence in those days.'

'Ah, Esther, that was a brief madness—a passing fever. While it lasted I was indeed hardly conscious of anything except my folly. Never speak to me of that time, Essie. I want to forget it altogether. I want to put it out of my power to look back upon it. I want to blot it out of my book of life.'

'Lady Perriam is free now. You might win her after all,' said Esther, lurking bitterness audible in her tones.

'I would not have her, polluted by falsehood. I would not take her stained by the memory of her treason against me. No, Esther, I am not such a slave as you seem to think me. Lady Perriam's widowhood makes no difference to my feelings. Were she to usurp a man's right, and sue for my love, I would not yield it to her; I have put the thought of her out of my life for ever.'

'I am very glad to hear that—for your own sake. For I do not believe she was ever worthy of you.'

Edmund smoked for a minute or two before replying. 'No, Essie, she was not worthy of me,' he said at last, 'unworthy as I may be in many respects; for I was true, and she was false. But there is one woman I know who is more than worthy of me, who is worthy of the best and truest lover that ever lived. I wish I could think myself not unworthy of her.'

'Your new idol must be very exalted if you feel yourself so much below her in merit,' said Esther, trying to speak lightly.

'She is the gentlest and most simple-minded of women, yet I feel unworthy to ask for her heart, because I once suffered my fancy to be led astray by a worthless woman, when I ought to have found my happiness close at hand. Nay, Essie darling, I won't speak in parables any longer. It is you I love, you whose sweetness has healed my wounded heart. We have been very happy in our evening walks, Esther. Is there any reason, except my unworthiness, that we should not travel side by side to the end of life?'

The girl looked up at him shyly, yet with a steady light in her soft dark eyes.

'You are in no manner unworthy of me, Edmund,' she replied, 'but I will not accept less than your whole heart. I love you well enough to be your adopted sister all my life, yes, even to see you happy with another woman, and take comfort from the thought of your happiness. But if you offer me any other kind of love than a brother's I must have all or nothing. I will not have your heart if there is a corner of it that still belongs to Lady Perriam.'

'Why do you mention that odious name?' cried Edmund, angrily. 'Did not I tell you that I had put her out of my life—that for me there is no such person as Sylvia Perriam? Answer an honest man's honest question, Essie. Will you be my wife?'

The question was very plainly put. There was

no purple light of love here to glorify the ancient theme. Yet Edmund seemed thoroughly in earnest. His tones and looks were tender, and truthful; she who listened to him loved him too well not to be deeply moved.

'That is too serious a question to be answered hastily,' replied Esther, gravely. 'We are very happy as we are, Edmund. Let our peaceful life go on, and let your question remain unanswered a little longer, till you better know your own mind.'

'I cannot know my own mind better than I do now. I want this question settled at once, Essie. I want to feel that I have a purpose in life—something to look forward to—something to hope for—something to dream about. I thought, while the pain of Sylvia's desertion was new, that I could never hope again, never weave the old dream of wife and home, without which a man's life is but a dreary business at best. Providence has been kinder to me than I deserved, Essie. I have learned to hope again, to love again; and you have been my gentle teacher.'

'I never tried to set you such a lesson; at least, as regards the last part of the business,' answered Esther, blushingly. 'Auntie and all of us were anxious to see you hopeful, but I don't think any one thought——'

'You don't think any one thought,' echoed Edmund, laughing at the girl's embarrassment; 'I know that my mother never cherished a fonder hope than that you and I should be one. You wouldn't disappoint her, would you, Essie, you who love her so well?'

'I have no thought but of your happiness, Edmund. You mustn't marry me just to please Auntie. That would not be the way to make your own life happy.'

'My life cannot be otherwise than happy in your companionship, Essie. Long ago you were my ideal woman. Yes, when you were only a girl of sixteen. Then came that fatal dream, and my love was lured away from you. I know now what a false flame that was which led me over marshes of difficulty, only to land me in the slough of despond. Come, Esther, darling, you are too kind to refuse me forgiveness for a wrong that has cost me so dearly.'

'I have nothing to forgive, Edmund. I cannot blame you for finding Sylvia Carew more attractive than myself.'

'Then, if there is nothing to forgive, all is settled; and you will be my dear little wife.'

The cigar had been thrown away ere this, and Edmund's arm had drawn Esther's slender form to his side, just as in twilights gone by Sylvia had nestled against his shoulder.

' You mean yes, Esther,' said Edmund, trying to see her downcast eyes.

' You haven't even asked me if I love you.'

' Suppose I am daring enough to fancy you do, just a very little, homœopathically, and not allo-pathically.'

' I love you with all my heart,'· she answered, with ˌa little burst of feeling, feeling so long re-pressed that it gushed out in spite of her desire to be restrained, wise, thoughtful for her lover, rather than for herself. ' I have no wish but to make you happy.'

' There is only one way of doing that, Essie. Be my wife. The sooner the better, sweet. I want to feel that I have an interest in life, that I have some one to work for. I hope you mean to be very ex-travagant, Essie, and spend all your money upon yourself, so that I may have to work hard for our children. Now, darling, it's getting dark and cold. I hope I haven't detained you here too long. But it was the business of a lifetime we had to settle, even at the risk of rheumatism or influenza. Come, love, do you know that is the best cigar I ever smoked.'

They went home together, happy, through the deepening night. How could Esther doubt her lover when he had so little doubt of himself?

CHAPTER XXII.

MR. BAIN IS PUZZLED.

It had been the popular belief at Hedingham and
Monkhampton that Lady Perriam's first use of her
liberty would be to take flight from the splendid
seclusion of ' the Place; ' but to the surprise and
even disappointment of these false prophets, who
would have liked to see their vaticinations realized,
Lady Perriam still continued to occupy the gloomy
old rooms, and to take her lonely walks in the Italian
garden.   She had youth, beauty, liberty, wealth;
all the world invited her to share its pleasures
while the bloom was still upon her life; yet she was
constant to the dreary existence she had lived with
her sick husband, and seemed proof against the
temptations which allure youth.

Even Mr. Bain wondered, and was not slow to
express his wonderment at her solitary and secluded
existence.   He saw her looking pale, and even care-

worn, as if with sleepless nights, and urged the necessity of change of air and scene.

' You ought to spend a few weeks at Weston-super-Mare or Malvern,' said the land steward, during one of his periodical visits to the Place: visits which Sylvia did her best to discourage, but which Mr. Bain continued as regularly as if he had received the warmest welcome. The Court of Chancery had made him guardian of the infant heir, according to the express wish of Sir Aubrey, as recorded in his will, Lady Perriam having no one she could put forward against him. He was thus, for all practical purposes, master of the house she lived in. He could come and go as he pleased; and she felt that his power had been increased, instead of being diminished, by her husband's death.

She made her stand against him, however, and without actually defying him did her best to resist his growing power.

' You are extremely kind, Mr. Bain,' she said, when the steward suggested change of air, ' but when I want advice I will take it from Mr. Stimpson.'

' But you are looking ill, must be ill, I should think, and you don't call in Stimpson.'

' When I want him I shall send for him.'

' Very well, Lady Perriam. Of course I have no right to interfere beyond the warm interest I feel in all that concerns you.'

Sylvia drew herself up haughtily at this speech.

' Be good enough to confine your interest to my son's affairs,' she said. ' The Court of Chancery did not appoint you my guardian.'

' I cannot be interested in the son without some anxiety about the mother. For St. John's sake you are bound to take care of your health. You are ruining your health, and even injuring your beauty, by the dismal life you lead here.'

That expression, ' injuring your beauty,' struck home. Lady Perriam looked in her glass directly Mr. Bain was gone, to see if he had told her the truth.

Yes, there was no doubt of it. She had a faded look already; her eyes were hollow, and their brightness was not the liquid lustre of happy youth, but a feverish brilliancy. She had a look of Mrs. Carter. She tossed off the light widow's cap impatiently, pushed back the thick hair from her forehead, and looked at herself with a searching scrutiny.

' Yes, there are wrinkles coming already, she

said, ' already, and I am not three-and-twenty. I think too much. I want rest of mind, change of scene. That man is right. His watchful eyes see everything. I wonder they don't read my inmost heart. He is right. I want change, fresher air to blow the faded look out of my face. But how can I ever leave this hateful house ? '

Mr. Bain went home ruminating upon that brief conversation with Lady Perriam. He had perceived her startled look, fleeting as the expression was, when he spoke of her faded beauty.

' She wants to preserve her good looks,' he thought. ' Is it for Edmund Standen's sake, I wonder ? '

A change had come upon the respectable dwelling in Monkhampton High-street, and this time the change was permanent. There was no further cause for the fluctuations of hope and fear. The mourning band which Mr. Bain had put round his hat after Sir Aubrey Perriam's death had been replaced by a deeper band which covered the hat almost to the top. Shadrach Bain was a widower. Mrs. Bain had revived considerably in the milder climate of Cannes. Her health, indeed, had so much improved as to renew hope in Clara Louisa's breast ; but just when she gave most hopeful accounts of the invalid, there came a sharp and sudden attack, which swept away this frail life.

Long as their minds had been divided by hope and fear, this event was a terrible shock for all the sons and daughters. Ill-health had become, in a manner, their mother's normal state. They had grown accustomed to think of her as an invalid, but they had never prepared themselves for her loss. Deepest sorrow and deepest gloom descended upon the comfortable orderly household. The jingle of the housekeeping keys, the pride of being mistress of her father's house, gave Matilda Jane no pleasure. The absence of the gentle house-mother made too sad a blank in the home.

Mr. Bain took his loss very quietly. People said he felt it all the more. But if his grief was deep it was not a vehement or passionate sorrow. His countenance, always serious and thoughtful, had a graver look now. He walked with downcast eyes, as if meditating upon the things of an unseen world. He became somewhat less regular in his attendance at the lengthy services in Water-lane Chapel. Whereon the Water-lane Chapelites, charitably disposed to a man of Mr. Bain's standing, told one another that the poor dear man could not bear to sit in the family pew without his wife.

In the cemetery, just outside Monkhampton, a handsome stone memorial, of the square and solid order, an obelisk with a flame at the top, which looked rather more like a landmark for distant navigators than a tribute of affection to the dead, already testified Mr. Bain's devotion to his departed spouse. There had been no delay—the order had been given to the mason the day after the funeral—the handsomest monument he could supply for a hundred pounds.

After a month or so the land steward's household returned to its normal state of methodical comfort. Matilda Jane had been too well drilled by the departed housewife to forget her teaching. Her eye was as keen as her mother's to scan the items in the butcher's book, and to detect a miscast of a column, or an error in the reckoning of ounces. Her hand was as steady as her mother's to weigh the grocery, and never made the servants' weekly half-pound of tea too light or too heavy. The two domestics allowed that Miss Bain was just, though, if anything, closer than her mamma.

Now that home had lost its chief charm in the removal of a fond and faithful wife, Mr. Bain might be forgiven if he spent less of his leisure by the domestic hearth than he had been wont to spend of old. He rode more, and devoted more time to the inspection of the Perriam property. Not a broken hurdle or a loosened drain pipe escaped that piercing eye. He took a good deal of trouble about small improvements, especially on that part of the land in which Lady Perriam had a life interest. ' If it were his own property,' said the gossips, ' Mr. Bain couldn't be more careful of it.'

Twice in every week he called at Perriam Place; saw Lady Perriam, inquired after the health of his ward, and, if possible, saw that small individual, who was apt to squall vindictively at sight of the guardian to whom the High Court of Chancery had confided his infant years. ' It's a pity,' nurse Tringfold said, ' but Sir St. John doesn't take to Mr. Bain, and can't be made to take to him.'

Sylvia reluctantly endured the steward's visits, and, though she always resisted his interference, she was nevertheless compelled to submit to it. He superintended all the details of the household, or, as the servants said, ' he had a finger in every pie.'

One day, soon after that evening walk upon Cropley Common which had united Edmund and Esther with the sacred bond of betrothal, Mr. Bain took occasion to make some inquiries about Mrs. Carter.

' Why do you keep that woman, Lady Perriam ? ' he asked. ' She is a very costly servant—I was surprised to find what heavy wages you pay her— and she can hardly be of any use now.'

' She is a great deal of use,' replied Sylvia, ' and I have no intention of dismissing her.'

The agent shrugged his shoulders, and gave Lady Perriam that keen look she both feared and hated. Her cheek had paled at his question. Was it anger that sent the sensitive blood from that fair cheek ?

' Don't be angry, Lady Perriam. Of course I've no right to interfere, but——'

' Some people are fond of interfering without right,' returned Sylvia, sharply. She was generally beaten in her battles with Mr. Bain, yet she never succumbed without a struggle.

' But I take a natural interest in your affairs,' continued the agent calmly, without any notice of the interruption, ' and I don't like to see you do anything foolish—out of good nature. For my own part I never keep more cats than can catch mice, and I really don't see what earthly use this Carter woman can be to you.'

' Perhaps you will kindly remember that she began life as a lady, and call her Mrs. Carter instead of " this Carter woman." '

'I'll be as deferential as you like, Lady Perriam. But you haven't told me why you keep her.'

'She is useful to me in more ways than one. First and foremost, she nurses Mr. Perriam when he is out of sorts.'

'But if Mr. Perriam is ill enough to want a nurse he ought surely to have the attendance of a medical man. Stimpson should take him in hand.'

'Mordred is not ill enough to require Mr. Stimpson; but his head is a little queer now and then. Mrs. Carter has more influence over him than any one, and can soothe him, as she used to soothe poor Sir Aubrey.'

'Yes, she is a clever woman. I always fancy those clever women with their soothing ways have a touch of the serpent in their composition.'

'I trust Mrs. Carter, and I like her, so you may suppose that she is not a serpent.'

'But you are so innocent, Lady Perriam; any one might take you in. I'm sorry poor Mr. Mordred is so queer. He ought to come out of his hole oftener, get more fresh air, see the world a little, in short. It's enough to addle any man's brain to be shut up in two rooms from one week's end to the other.'

' Mr. Perriam has never cared to leave his rooms since his brother's death. Pray don't suggest that doctors should see him. They might urge us to put him into a lunatic asylum. He is only a harmless, half-imbecile old man. He is well off as he is.'

' Very well, Lady Perriam. I will not interfere. Nothing pleases me better than to obey your wishes, if you will only express them plainly.'

' Then I wish Mordred Perriam to be let alone, and not to be troubled by Mr. Stimpson or any other doctor.'

' So be it, as long as his bodily health gives no cause for alarm. We must not let him die for want of medical care.'

' He is not likely to die yet awhile,' said Lady Perriam, with something like a regretful sigh, as if Mordred's existence were just a little burdensome. ' He is well cared for by Mrs. Carter, and he is as happy as he can be, allowing for his natural grief for the loss of his brother.'

This settled the matter. For once the land steward was conquered. Indeed, his manner of late had been more deferential than usual. He seemed, as he declared himself, only anxious to please Lady Perriam in all things.

He was not a little disturbed by the thought of this interview with Sylvia as he rode slowly homewards. He had never liked Mrs. Carter. Her placid countenance and her repose of manner worried him, for he fancied that beneath that smooth exterior she concealed an active intellect, and perchance a plotting brain, a brain that might counterplot his own secret plans. He would have given much to get her away from Perriam Place, powerless as she must be compared with himself. But he now perceived that it was vain to think of getting rid of her. She had some hidden influence, some firm hold upon Sylvia Perriam.

'There is something,' thought Shadrach Bain, 'some secret between those two women. I could read as much in Lady Perriam's face to-day, when it paled at the mention of Mrs. Carter's name. Is the link a secret of the remote past, before Sylvia was Sir Aubrey's wife? Or has it something to do with the time I was away, just before Sir Aubrey's death? There was a strangeness in Lady Perriam's manner when I first saw her after her husband's death which I have never been able to explain to myself. I have not forgotten her look of horror when we went into Sir Aubrey's room. A woman's natural horror of death, perhaps. Yet she seems of too stern a metal

for weak fears such as those.   There is something—
a secret—a mystery somewhere, and that woman
Carter knows all about it.   Why should I puzzle my
brains to unravel it?   Whatever it is I'll make it
work into the web of my own scheme, or I am something less than Shadrach Bain.'

END OF VOL. II.

Woodfall and Kinder, Printers, Milford Lane, Strand, London, W.C.

www.ingramcontent.com/pod-product-compliance
Lightning Source LLC
Chambersburg PA
CBHW031028120726
47905CB00007B/2095